BILLOWTAIL

Sherry Boas

Caritas Press, USA

"A delightful story that quickly captures the reader's interest, sparks the imagination and, without being preachy, leads one to a deeper sense of the mystery of creation. I recommend it for kids and adults."

—The Most Reverend Thomas J. Olmsted
Bishop of Phoenix

FOR MY CHILDREN, who inspire me in so many ways: MARIA with her love for animals and keen sense of humor; MICHAEL with his kind and gentle way reminiscent of St. Francis; TERESA with her profound appreciation of all things cute; and JOHN with his inexhaustible imagination and insatiable appetite for adventure.

CONTENTS

CHAPTER ONE

THE FALL OF PUTTERMUNCH

SQUIRRELS WERE NOT DESIGNED for this sort of thing. Everybody knew that. Nobody knew it better than Billowtail. Each furlong yielded a bigger bulge of blister. Do not misunderstand. His hands and feet were not unaccustomed to rough wear, thanks to many a tree scaled with and against gravity. But they were proving less than ideal for covering large horizontal distances necessary for the epic journey he had been pressed into.

Billowtail would have been happy to live his entire life alone, within a fathom of his drey, but when the accident happened, it seemed he had no choice but to go, for the sake of the wee Puttermunch and the poor baby squirrel's grieving mother.

And so, Billowtail found himself crossing an unending mountain range, who knows how far from home, with four other squirrels. Sir Sniff was close behind him. Nip was ahead between him and Tippy. At the lead was Sugarcoat. She wasn't in the lead because she was necessarily the fastest, but because she had ordered Tippy and Nip to stay behind her. It was uncertain what the two young squirrels would do unsupervised, especially Tippy, who had very creative ideas that always seemed unwise in hindsight. Nip did not have those kinds of ideas, but he always seemed to like Tippy's and would often, quite unwisely, join in their execution. So it was perhaps fitting that Tippy and Nip were known back home as troublemakers, though their goal was never to make trouble. It was unlikely they had any kind of goal at all, actually, except to seek fun.

Sugarcoat happened to mention that she overheard a fellow traveler on this route remark that he was so high up, he could touch the sky. Tippy took this as in invitation to try it. He walked a good league up on his toes, arms stretched to the sky. Nip finally pushed Tippy's arms back down by his sides, reminding him that it had been quite a number of weeks since he had a bath.

"You don't want us all to go unconscious and roll off this mountain, do you, Tippy?" Nip teased.

There was no registry of that question on Tippy's part. Tippy's arms sprang back up and Billowtail began to imagine that maybe Tippy's fingertips just might be skimming the surface of the sky. Wishing to feel what vibrant blue hope feels like to the tips of your fingers, Billowtail lifted his hands tentatively above his head as well, looking around self-consciously, hoping no one would notice, and if they did, that they wouldn't say anything. He could not feel anything at the tips of his fingers, but he did feel something within him. He felt suddenly tall, which is something a squirrel never feels. Out there in the wide expanse on the top of the wide green mountain, with nothing but a dome above, no trees to make him feel small, he came to wonder how big the world actually is and how big he might be within it. It was as if his mind were expanding into the expansive sky. He had never wondered such things before, and for a little while, the stretching of his mind was uncomfortable and disquieting. But he grew used to it and sort of even liked it, and he continued to walk, arms extended until his biceps and triceps began to burn. It's hard to say how long that was, but it had to be a good amount of time, since squirrels are very fit in their arms due to frequent tree climbing and occasional branch swinging.

The five squirrels who called themselves *The Alliance* were headed over the Pyrenees because Sugarcoat had heard that the Great Pinky who had taken Puttermunch was bound for a place over the mountain called Roncesvalles in a country called Spain. None of the squirrels knew, before Sugarcoat acquired the magic thread, that they lived not too far from the Spanish border in a place called France. They made their home in the woods of Bon Arbre and never saw a Great Pinky up close, until the day the horseman unhitched his horse from his cart and went for a bareback ride through the woods with his bow and quiver full of arrows.

To say "horseman" is to use the term loosely. The horse was not much of one, sagging in the middle and long in the tooth, and the rider was quite small, and seemed to Billowtail to be not yet full-grown. Apart from size, it is very difficult to distinguish adult Great Pinkies from younglings. They are all pink and hairless, regardless of their age, whereas with squirrels, they only start off pink and hairless, quite different from the beautiful auburn or white or slate or ebony or golden-coated specimens they will become. It has always been a mystery that new mother squirrels aren't completely shocked by what pops out of them—squirming, fleshy, blind pinkies, who will bear no resemblance to their parents for a number of milk-fed weeks.

Sugarcoat had since learned that the "horseman" at Bon Arbre that day was actually thirteen years old, and that was considered somewhat young for a Great Pinky, whereas it is considered unusually elderly for a squirrel. (Four out of five squirrels don't even live to see their first birthday, so great are the treacheries of their fragile existence.)

Tired from an unsuccessful hunt, the boy beneath Mrs. Poggins' tree put away his bow, tied his horse, and opened his saddlebag to retrieve a barley loaf. He propped his back against the tree trunk, tore the bread, and stuffed it in his mouth. Hearing the rustling down below and wishing to pop her head out of the drey to investigate, Mrs. Poggins squeezed her way through her nest packed with tiny warm and pink bodies. At six, this was her largest litter to date and the drey was quite crowded. The newborn squirrels began to squirm at being disturbed in their sleep, and Mrs. Poggins tripped over one of their tails and fell to her face between two of them with a clumsy thud, displacing the pinkies right and left and pushing one of them right out of the nest. If it wasn't for the boy's open saddlebag which contained a rolled-up surcoat and provided a soft bed for landing, Puttermunch would have surely perished. And it was a good thing the boy was ravenously hungry or he might have left a portion of his barley loaf uneaten and returned it to his saddlebag, plopping it on top of Puttermunch, who would have been too helpless and weak to wriggle his way out from under it.

The rescue effort was assembled haphazardly, having no benefit of advance planning (since how does one plan for something like this?) and no large number of applicants to choose from. What Mrs. Poggins ended up with was this: Billowtail, a decent, reasonable golden fellow in his young adult years; Tippy, an adventurous and impulsive red-headed adolescent; Nip, a peer and emulator of Tippy minus, thankfully, a bit of the recklessness and creativity; Sir Sniff, a middle-aged gentleman possessing a fair amount of wisdom and physical stamina; and Sugarcoat, a determined, assertive and clever white squirrel, who could boast the longest tail in all the history of Bon Arbre (if she ever did boast, which she did not.)

It can be said, with all certainty, that none of the squirrels, who called themselves *The Alliance*, knew what they were in for. They had no idea they would have to travel so many miles. So many arduous miles. Since they had never left their small territory in the forest of Bon Arbre, they had no concept of what covering that great distance would mean.

In addition to blistered hands and feet, Billowtail's cheeks positively ached with fatigue. It is not common for tree squirrels to pack. As a matter of fact, it is simply not done. But Sheilagwen, the busybody of Bon Arbre, had somehow convinced Billowtail it could work, based on the fact it always worked for her, and chipmunks are not anatomically that unlike squirrels, at least in the minds of chipmunks. Although his nut stash back home was more voluminous than he had ever accomplished in past seasons, Billowtail had to leave all behind except what he could carry in his pathetic face-satchels. He may never regain the cheek elasticity to play his reed again. His belly rumbled with hollow anticipation of unpacking an acorn or two from his jaw, but his good judgment bid him to wait. His cheeks may have been carrying all the nourishment he was going to see for some time. Plus the unpacking and repacking, the cracking and shelling of the nut, and the actual consuming of it, would take time, and he would be left behind. One thing is for certain: his travel companions would not wait. Squirrels are solitary animals, and although the fellowship of five had been sent on a common mission, banding together goes against instinct, and they had no comprehension of the term used by the Great Pinkies: "safety in numbers." They also had no understanding of "breaking bread together." Alas, common mealtimes were out of the question for the road-weary rodents at this point. Anyway, it was imperative for Billowtail to keep up with the group, since Sugarcoat had possession of the magic thread, which allowed for the interpretation of the Great Pinkies' crude forms of communications they call "languages." It's a long story of how squirrels came to possess such a rare article, but for now suffice it to say that, without it, there would be little hope of picking up clues as to what had become of Mrs. Poggins' baby.

It is difficult not to presume Puttermunch lost forever. No one knows exactly how long a pinky can live without mother's milk. Everyone agrees it can't be long. But word on this route is that a couple of travelers were twittering about how cute and remarkable it was that a pilgrim's cat gave birth right in his nag-drawn cart and adopted a baby squirrel as a member of her litter. Oh what delicacy! The milk of a domesticated animal! Surely, if it is true, Puttermunch is destined for greatness. And if it is not true, Puttermunch has certainly left this world, even before his tail is fully fluffed.

The difficulty lies in not being able to ask any questions of the Great Pinkies since, magic thread or no magic thread, squirrel language sounds like nothing but the senseless chattering of a gossiping old woman to humans. The squirrels can only rely on what the men happen to be talking about to glean intelligence, and even then, only when Sugarcoat wears the thread around her tail or neck. It will be interesting to see how it will work on other species besides Great Pinkies. Billowtail had taken nothing for granted and had rehearsed in his head what charade he would employ to communicate with the mother cat when he finally found her.

He fancied she would view him as something of a hero if he could somehow get the story across to her. She would be impressed with his valor and his perseverance. It was a nice fantasy in which to revel for awhile. He looked forward to communicating to her, through a series of dramatic re-enactments, what he had overcome and overtaken. Squirrels are good at dramatics, and they enjoy it. It's the tail. It would be difficult to be demure or retiring with such a flamboyant thing attached to your backside. The tail is a superb punctuator. A splendid conveyor of emotion. It also serves other non-dramatic purposes as well. It is a blanket, a sunshade, an umbrella and a shield. It is a rudder and a counterbalance to the body when leaping from branch to branch.

Branch leaping is something Billowtail sorely missed. He had been on the ground too long, treading dust and dirt. It would have been tolerable for a ground squirrel. But tree squirrels were made for trees, and trees for tree squirrels. This is an undeniable fact that allows for the symbiotic existence between squirrel and tree. Trees provide food for squirrels, and squirrels ensure the survival of trees by planting tree seeds for generations of squirrels to come. They don't mean to do this, but sometimes they forget where they bury their acorns, and then the rain comes and the sun shines and the seed bursts and up pops a baby tree, which will grow up and make more acorns to feed more squirrels, who will also bury some of them and forget where they put them.

Billowtail thought Spain could use a few more squirrels with memory loss. It is said that the country has so much forest, a squirrel can cross it by jumping from tree to tree, without ever touching the ground. This is wholesale fable. There certainly never seems to be a trunk within running distance when a barker decides he needs a little nourishment. Just yesterday, Billowtail had no choice but to bolt straight for the thing that looked, to him, most like a tree trunk. He scurried up the coarse and tattered brown robe of a Great Pinky to narrowly escape becoming a tasty morsel for a ravenous hound. The smiling, bearded man harbored Billowtail in the crook of his arm as he bent to eye-level of the charging dog, which immediately dissolved in a limp, quivering mound of furry adulation and offered his underbelly to be scratched.

Oh, all the safety and comfort of Bon Arbre, never appreciated before, created a profound longing deep in Billowtail's heart. He craved familiarity. And snacks. Even in the best of times, it is difficult for a squirrel to resist stopping to slurp at some sap. Billowtail couldn't help but notice, on a passing tree, that some chisel-toothed creature had already scraped the bark and made the tree ooze, and the perfect amount of time had passed to evaporate the perfect amount of water, making for the perfect liquid confection. How he wished to run his tongue over it and lap it into his parched mouth, letting the sweetness coat the back of his throat and seep to the pit of his growling gut.

That's what a squirrel is made for. He is certainly not made for the road. Billowtail assumed there would be an end to these mountains – that at some point, he would be descending onto flat land and at some point that land would offer a tree. Not that the beauty of the mountain range was lost on him—the way the clouds hung in the empty spaces out there in the distance and even up close. But he missed the closed-in coziness of trees. The open spaces were beginning to give him a lonely homesickness.

Sure enough and finally, the road began to descend, and Billowtail's gloom was interrupted by a yelp of optimism.

"Look!" yelled Nip, who was now about twenty paces ahead of Tippy, who was (disobediently) fifteen paces ahead of Sugarcoat, who was ten paces ahead of Billowtail, who was five paces ahead of Sir Sniff. Nip had stopped and the rest of the squirrels ran to his side, arriving at various intervals to revel at the sight down below: cart and horse parked next to a stone structure which none of the squirrels could name, since none had ever seen anything quite like it in Bon Arbre, although it did bear a resemblance to something Sugarcoat had heard about and she surmised it might be one of those. A chapel is what they called it, if this indeed was what they were looking at.

"The boy! The boy!" Tippy yelled, jumping up and down. The squirrels watched as the boy returned to his cart to retrieve something large enough to see from all that distance, but too small to determine what it was.

"Let it be, oh please let it be!" cried Nip, squinting into the hope that lay before them.

Billowtail clasped his hands together and tried to ignore the pain of blister pressing against blister. "Let there be a baby squirrel in that cart."

CHAPTER TWO

OLIPHANT TALES

W ELL, WHAT ARE WE WAITING FOR?" Nip yelled, taking off into the village. All the squirrels ran after him, with Sugarcoat barking warnings about being too conspicuous. "Slow down," she grumbled, "and be quiet. There is not a speck of subtlety in the whole lot of you."

They did indeed slow their pace, as well as stifle their stomps when they got closer and realized the boy was not alone. He was on his way to join a gathering of travelers refreshing themselves at the river. The squirrels found some suitably tall rushes to hide in, trying to see if perhaps the boy had taken the cat from the cart to let her drink. The squirrels certainly did not want to approach the cart if she was still inside. They did not know much about cats, but they were savvy enough to know that squirrels are somewhere near the bottom of the food chain, and they were pretty sure any animal larger would be above them. Sugarcoat took the opportunity, while hiding and watching, to put the magic thread to good use and try to glean as much information as she could from the Great Pinkies' odd language.

Maybe lacking an official minstrel or maybe because there was little else to do on long journeys, the Great Pinkies took spontaneous turns entertaining each other. The boy himself played the bagpipe, and there was a big, round happy fellow who played a fiddle. The others told stories, whose meaning eluded Sugarcoat. Though she understood each word, the words just didn't make much sense when they were put together. She was very good, however, at interpreting practical matters.

When it was the turn of the older gentleman with the well-worn surcoat, he explained to the half dozen, who had come to rest under a shade tree after having a drink from the river, that there was room for all of them to stay the night in a place called a monastery. The boy seemed very happy. He told the man it would be his first night in a bed in many, many days. The monastery was famous for its kindness to travelers who called themselves "pilgrims." Thanks to donations from the wealthy, the monks had the means to treat pilgrims well and fed as many as thirty thousand travelers in some years. Sugarcoat could not determine where all these travelers were from or where they were headed, but it was clear, they were all bound for the same place, and for some reason, folks at the monastery wanted to make their journey a little easier.

"The door lies open to all," the old man bellowed with joy as a smile grew wide across the boy's face. "To sick and strong. To Catholic and pagan. To idler and vagabond. To good and bad, sacred and profane."

Billowtail wondered, as Sugarcoat relayed that message to The Alliance, if squirrels fell into any of those categories. He would very much like a good meal.

"The story teller also said this place is famous for a legendary battle between the Franks and the Moors," said Sugarcoat.

"Who are they?" asked Tippy.

"I am not certain," said Sugarcoat, "but this fellow named Roland, said to be the nephew of the great emperor Charlemagne, was riding his horse, right here in this place where we stand right now. Or close to it. He was carrying his sounding horn called an oliphant and his unbreakable sword named Durendal through Roncesvalles Pass when he and his troops were ambushed after his stepfather betrayed him and told the enemy where to find him."

"Could Durendal not save him?" Tippy wanted to know.

"Did the enemy have a stronger sword?" Nip asked.

"It was not the sword that did him in," said Sugarcoat. "No, it was pride."

"Pride?" asked Billowtail.

"His advisor begged him to call for help from Charlemagne's army, but he refused, believing he could handle it himself. But when almost all his men were dead, he blew his elephant tusk so hard, his temples burst."

"Temples? What are temples?" Tippy asked.

"The sides of the forehead," said Sir Sniff. "That flat part that feels a bit squishy when you push on it."

"Do squirrels have temples?" Nip asked, pressing on the sides of his head with his fingertips.

"Why, yes, I think we do," said Sir Sniff.

"They can burst?" asked Billowtail, thinking of all the times he blew very hard on his reed and hoping somehow that's different from blowing into an elephant's tusk, but vowing not to blow so hard in the future.

"Well, that is how the French legend goes in a famous story called the *Song of Roland*," said Sugarcoat.

"Poor Mr. Roland," said Tippy.

"Why did he sing about it?" asked Nip. "I thought songs were for happy things."

"Perhaps it is called the *Song of Roland* because of the tune that came out of his oliphant when he blew it to call for help," reasoned Sir Sniff.

"Is that a true story?" Nip asked, skeptically.

"Well, the storytellers insist that's how the story goes," said Sugarcoat.

True or not, The Alliance might have learned a lesson from Roland they could have used later. But squirrels are not accustomed to gleaning morals from literature.

"Anyway," said Sir Sniff, "We best return our attentions to the business at hand – finding poor

Puttermunch. Since it seems the boy has an indoor bed tonight, he will be leaving his cart unattended for an extended period of time for the first time since we began our journey. Then, we will just have to determine what to do about mother cat."

The squirrels watched and waited for dark, from a distance, behind a large rock. Billowtail's stomach let out a loud rumble, and he remembered that, aside from a caterpillar plucked from a leaf that happened to be hanging in his path, he had not eaten a thing all day. He had food, just no time to eat it. He was beginning to think that Sir Sniff had spoken wisely when he said to leave all behind. Billowtail had come to understand that the pain of carrying food in his face was worse that the hunger pains in his belly. He decided to eat as much as he could from what came out of his cheeks and bury the rest behind a big rock so he could collect it on his way back through.

As the lightning bugs lit up, the squirrels saw the boy placing one thing after another in a beaten leather scrip bag. They couldn't get a good look in the dusky light, at what exactly was going into the bag, but they presumed it to be four kittens and a baby squirrel, as they heard mewing, and at one point, the boy held one of the objects to his cheek.

"There now, you will be warm tonight," he said. "And so will I."

He gently placed the strap over his shoulder and entered into the warm orange glow of the monastery door, mother cat padding behind.

CHAPTER THREE

RUNNING WITH BULLS

BILLOWTAIL WISHED so badly they could have gotten a glimpse of Puttermunch. No one even knew if he was still alive. The cart was empty when Billowtail and Sir Sniff went to investigate after all the Great Pinkies had gone to bed. The squirrels were assuming he was still among the kittens. They had nothing but hope to fuel their perseverance. Fortunately, hope comes naturally to a squirrel, so it wasn't hard for The Alliance to take to the road the next morning, when the boy loaded his cart, gave his horse a drink, filled his canteen with river water and set out on his way.

He did not stop even to eat, grabbing an apple from his bag and consuming it while his horse pressed on. It was grueling for the squirrels to travel without any breaks, but they somehow made it without losing sight of the cart even once, darting through tall grasses, behind bushes and trees. A village—much larger than the last one—came into view right at sunset. The squirrels gave into exhaustion and fell fast asleep in a tree above the cart, where the boy curled up under a blanket and settled in for the night.

It was mysterious how, not just one of the squirrels, and not just two, but every one of them, out-slept the boy, and when they awoke the next morning, he was gone. If they had been anyone but squirrels, they might have thought of taking turns staying awake to keep watch. But a squirrel just sleeps when a squirrel is tired, unless there is someone about to eat him.

The village was overtaken by a bustle of noise and movement, large gatherings of people buying and selling. Jugglers, musicians, loud merchants and eager shoppers seemed to be full of the same kind of energy squirrels have when they are gathering and storing.

The squirrels watched it all from their perch in a tree on the edge of the village green.

"How could he have gotten away?" asked Billowtail. "How could we have not heard him leave without us?"

"I just hope he hasn't gotten far," Sir Sniff said.

"What if he's gone on?" Billowtail fretted. "What if he's on the road again?"

"Hey, where is Sugarcoat?" asked Tippy.

"Oh no, now we have two squirrels to find," Nip lamented. "That means we're even farther from home."

"Why would Sugarcoat go off without telling us?" Sir Sniff worried. "I hope nothing's happened–"

"Nothing's happened," came a voice from below. "I was just taking a listen to the Great Pinkies to see where we are."

"Sugarcoat! Thank Heavens!" said Billowtail.

"Well, where are we?" asked Tippy.

"We are in a place called Pamplona," Sugarcoat reported. "All the activity here is called a fair. People are trying to get rid of some things and get other things, like little round shiny things. Everyone has brought their wares from many miles away. So, I'm thinking maybe the boy has something to get rid of too, and maybe he'll pitch a tent."

"We need to split up and cover the fair ground," said Billowtail. "Even if he isn't getting rid of anything, with any luck, maybe we will find him trying to get something."

"No," said Sugarcoat. "Let's stay together for now."

"Agreed," said Sir Sniff. "We can't afford to waste time looking for each other."

The squirrels tried to move about unnoticed but there was not much to hide them, especially since there were five of them. Fortunately, most Great Pinkies were distracted by each other and were not paying attention to the wildlife, particularly that at squirrel level.

"My eyes hurt," Tippy complained, stopping to rub them near the tent of a textile trader. The sights were all too rich for a country squirrel, whose usual color palette is green, brown and blue—leaves, trunk and sky. The fair burst with hues from faraway lands—vibrant silks, lush rugs and elaborate tapestries woven from threads of rare color. Every color, it seemed. And every color in between. It was difficult to even look at red for more than an eye bat or two.

"And my nostrils," complained Nip. The smells of the fair were to the nose what the kaleidoscope of color was to the eye. The multitude of various exotic spices, first one wafting past, then the next and then a combination of many, forming a composite of all new smells. This is the kind of thing many find intoxicating about fairs, but for a squirrel who has been used to sniffing the same three acres of wood since the day he was born, it was quite unnerving.

"Come on," said Billowtail. "Let's just hurry and find Puttermunch so we can go home."

"I am for that," said Sir Sniff. "My ears are killing me."

The noisiest thing back home was the chirping of crickets breaking through the evening stillness and the variety of song birds warming up their voices in the soft light of morning. But the fair was a constant din of barkers (not referring to the four-legged variety, but the name the Great Pinkies give to other Great Pinkies who yell at them to buy things.) Also making a considerable amount of noise were the buyers haggling for a lower price and the musicians and storytellers vying for admiration (and coinage) from the next passerby.

But Billowtail had scampered on a few paces and found something to delight his ears—something like a bird's song, but so much sweeter, if you can believe that. As he got closer, he saw it was a man, blowing into a flute. The sound made him miss his reed back home, and he made a silent vow to make playing it the second thing he does when he returns to Bon Arbre. The first, of course, would be to hug his tree for as long as it would take to realize that "home" is not just a dream, but a real and actual place. He had dreamed about Bon Arbre every night since they left. The strange thing is, he could not recall ever having a dream before that, although he had heard other squirrels talk about dreams of eating giant acorns and nightmares involving ravenous wolves "hatching" out of giant acorns.

A small group of others stood around the man making that beautiful music, smiles on their lips, peace in their eyes. He was different from other men, somehow. He didn't move the same way. He seemed stiffer than most. If you would see that sort of mannerism on a squirrel, you would understand that the squirrel had thrown his back out carrying too heavy a cache of nuts, or had misstepped while swinging from one branch to another, plummeting to the ground and landing tail first in a raspberry patch. The man, in a certain way, reminded Billowtail of a newborn pinky. The jerking sudden movements. The head searching for some point of reference that the eyes cannot provide because the eyes have not yet turned on.

That's it! That's what was different about this man playing the flute. He was blind! Billowtail stole up ever closer to the glorious sound. He wanted to have it in his ears forever, and maybe somewhere inside him, he believed that if he could get close enough, he could hold and possess it, like a string of pearls waiting to be snatched from the air, though Billowtail never would have put it in those terms since no one in Bon Arbre had ever seen a pearl, much less a string of them. The people must have thought the flute song a treasure as well since the blind minstrel's cap was filling up with half-pennies and pennies, which Sugarcoat soon learned, are used for obtaining things you want. If squirrels wanted anything other than nuts, I suppose they would have been quite unhappy that they never had any silver. But nuts were free, as long as you could find them, as long as there were fruitful trees. All it took was some harvesting. Now, it is quite possible that if squirrels ever did have any currency, they wouldn't mind having a few luxuries, like a little bit of olive oil to rub on their paws to soothe the abrasions or some trinket made of yew to aid in the shortening of their teeth. (Yew is the perfect gnawing wood for several reasons. It is very hard and resistant to splitting due to its interlocked grains, reducing the chance of lip splinters. It is also weatherproof, which means saliva will not harm it.)

In any event, Billowtail was happy for the blind minstrel. He seemed to be making out alright. It seemed the merriment of the fair had put everyone into good spirits, and amicable moods often foster generosity. This was true even among the squirrels, who passed around crumbs fallen from foods brought to the fair from the four corners and dropped by Great Pinkies, who tend to be quite slobbish at fairs.

Ordinarily, it is unheard of for squirrels to share. They work hard for their nuts and they never know when and how hungry they might be in the future. Not only is sharing typically out of the question, but it is common, sorry to say, for squirrels to steal from each other. That is why a squirrel will dig several holes for each nut. Some of the holes are decoys, meant to frustrate the thief when he digs and digs and comes up empty. Sometimes the hider even fools himself. As often as humans misplace the mate to their sock, squirrels forget where they put their nuts.

But there was no angst, at the moment, for the squirrels, who were lulled by the sweet music and tasty crumbs into a sense of well-being that could have made them forget why they had come. Then, a man wearing a gray tunic and white coif sauntered up to the hat full of coins, and looking uneasily around him, grabbed the hat, shoved it under his tunic and took off running. *"Stop! Thief!"* someone yelled and one person and then another swiped at him in an effort to restrain him, but he was able to slip through their fingers like he was made of air. Billowtail was the first of the five squirrels to take off running after the man, but soon they were all in dogged pursuit of him. It must have been a strange sight, maybe never witnessed before or since. A gangling, skinny peasant, running from a band of fluff-tailed vigilantes, single file, starting with Billowtail and followed by Sugarcoat and then Tippy, then Nip, then Sniff. The thief dared not look back after that initial moment when he glanced over his shoulder and had to glance yet again to confirm what he had seen. He hoofed through the fair, overturning a table of Byzantine silk and tripping on a bushel basket of bright yellow quinces, which rolled in twenty-two different directions. The squirrels had to jump over the fruits to keep from being bowled over. For the most part, the strategy worked quite well and they lost little time, until Billowtail failed to clear one of them fast enough and took it right in the gut, knocking the wind out of him and sending him to the ground momentarily. Sugarcoat, Nip and Sir Sniff looked back and kept running. Tippy doubled back to pick Billowtail up off the ground.

"I'm OK," said Billowtail, struggling to regain his breath. "C'mon, we're going to lose him. Where did he go?"

There was no sign of the thief or the squirrels. "They must have rounded a corner," said Tippy in a panic.

He and Billowtail ran in the direction they had last seen the thief heading and soon spotted their friends chasing after the thief through a side alley. By taking the diagonal across the fair grounds, Tippy and Billowtail were able to cut off a sizable amount of distance and catch up with their cohorts.

The thief, being resourceful as thieves often are, happened to notice a pen of cattle, waiting to be sold at market. He doubled back and quickly unlatched the gate, setting free a massive amount of bovine weight and power, all of which came barreling down the road at the five squirrels. Knowing they could not turn and outrun the bulls, the squirrels leaped into the air and landed on the backs of the snorting beasts, running in the opposite direction, from nose to tail, nose to tail, nose to tail, and jumping off when the very last bull had passed under them.

All except one squirrel, that is.

Billowtail, realizing the bulls and steers were headed straight for a crowd of Great Pinkies, mostly little ones who might be children, decided to remain on top of one of the bulls, holding onto its ear to keep from flying off. At intervals, Billowtail's feet would leave the bull and he would be flapping in the wind like a flag. He was determined to ride this herd of bulls until everyone was out of harm's way. He felt partly responsible for whatever might happen next since, if it wasn't for him, there wouldn't have been a high-speed pursuit of the thief, who felt desperate enough to release the bulls. Much to Billowtail's surprise, a number of Great Pinkies began to run alongside the bulls and several ran ahead, in an effort to entice the thunderous herd to follow. It worked beautifully and the dozen or so men, along with the "help" of one squirrel, were able to corral the entire herd into the arena where the bulls would be shown for sale.

A round of applause went up among the crowd, and a number of people made unexpected comments which Sugarcoat later translated as the squirrels refreshed themselves in a fountain.

"We should do this every year!" one man who had taken up the chase exclaimed.

"Yes, let's make a tradition of this running with the bulls."

That's when Billowtail understood how different this species they call man is from squirrel. No normal being would say such a thing. Squirrels are positively logical in all circumstances, throughout all ages, in all corners of creation.

And that is why Billowtail was surprised and perplexed by his own instinct to want to save the small Great Pinkies. He had a hard time thinking the Billowtail of Bon Arbre would have done such a thing. But, here, the Billowtail of the road did not think twice. Though they were no closer to finding Puttermunch, and the thief had escaped, The Alliance was feeling proud to have, at least, given him a run for his ill-gotten money.

CHAPTER FOUR

LADY FLORA

A S MENTIONED EARLIER, squirrels are not naturally benevolent creatures, but one of the most generous moments in squirrel history was about to unfold.

It was decided that, having covered most of the fairgrounds, perhaps The Alliance should begin to look for the boy in outlying areas.

After making a sweeping circle around the property, the squirrels stopped in a thicket of trees to enjoy some shade and grab a bite to eat. Sir Sniff sensed they were standing on top of a field of buried nuts. They all began to dig and bring up various varieties of dinner – acorns, maple seed "helicopters" and young and tender, petite pinecones. The squirrels were all so hungry, they failed to notice there was someone watching them from an overhead tree branch.

"What do you think you're doing?" came the rhetorical, yet startling question.

"Oh, uh, oh," stammered Billowtail, holding tighter to his acorn. "We, uh, we, we—"

"Do those nuts belong to you?" the voice from above persisted.

"We see no markings that prove ownership of this food," said Sugarcoat up into the branches. "So we are dining here tonight."

"What?" It wasn't just the statement that threw the stranger off. It was the "we." The idea that the squirrels invading her territory were a unified front. It was quite disturbing. Not just because she was outnumbered, but because a squirrel had actually used the first person plural. It would be like watching the constellations move backwards across the sky or seeing geese fly upside down. The universe doesn't allow for such things. Neither does it allow for a band of squirrels. But there they were, descending on her nuts and other goodies, with winter's hunger looming on her horizon.

Truth be told, Billowtail had a strange, uneasy feeling about taking food that didn't belong to him. He never had such a feeling before, but this journey had wrought something foreign in him. Something disquieting and a bit uncomfortable.

"Well, I guess I can't stop you," said the owner of the nuts scampering to a higher branch. "You are more squirrels than I am. But I would appreciate if you would all refrain from gluttony. I might not survive the winter."

"I am sorry," Sir Sniff said. "We are just very hungry. We have been traveling a long way."

"Ravenous actually," said Billowtail, pushing the words out through a mouth full of acorn.

"Where have you travelled from?" the owner of the nuts asked, still not showing herself. "Which tree?"

32

"We come from a very distant tree, one that is too far to see. We have come over mountains, rivers and field."

"Why?" she said aghast. "Why would you do such a thing?"

Billowtail was thinking about a good answer to that question as he dug deep into the moist soil. "Oh, not there, please," the stranger begged. "Please do not dig there."

But it was too late. Billowtail had almost completely unearthed the biggest pinecone he had ever laid eyes on. Everyone else had gathered round to gawk. "Oh, oh, oh dear. Would you mind very much, please, if I could keep that particular pinecone?" The squirrel finally came down and made herself completely visible. She was a compact sort, with a petite but perfectly formed tail and the longest ear tufts Billowtail had ever seen. They were auburn, like her hands and feet, which looked quite fancy on a predominantly white squirrel. "I have been saving it for a special occasion."

Billowtail wanted so badly to sink his teeth into the wood petals and rip them off, exposing what he was sure would be the tastiest, most colossal pine nuts known to squirrel. "OK," Billowtail conceded. "There's plenty of other food here. But where did you get such a pinecone as this?"

The others went back to resume where they had left off, digging and gnawing.

"It's a long story," said the stranger. "But I will make an exchange with you. A story for a story. I want to hear your tale. What on earth would possess you to leave your home?"

"We are in search of a baby, who fell from his nest," said Billowtail, "into the saddlebag of someone the Great Pinkles call a pilgrim."

"Are you his father?" she asked, sauntering back up the tree.

Billowtail laughed nervously at the thought of someone thinking he could be a father. The journey must have aged him, he reasoned.

"No," he said. "Puttermunch doesn't belong to any of us. He is the seventeenth offspring of Mrs. Penelope Poggins."

The stranger's face froze, ears up, eyes wide, as if sensing a tremor deep in the earth that would, before long, shake the world and all its living things.

"You have come all this way looking for a pinky that is not even your own?" Her face softened now and her eyes became larger, rounder and more luminous, and Billowtail thought a tear might fall from one of them. "I have never heard of such a thing." She ripped a leaf from the branch and dabbed at her eyes with it and then let it float to the ground. She walked head first down the trunk of the tree and scurried to her prized pinecone, which Billowtail had done his best to re-bury. She dipped her fingers into the dirt, lifted the pinecone out, brought it to Billowtail and raised it toward his face. "Here," she said, craning her head to look around it.

"What? No. I couldn't. Really."

"This is a special occasion," she said, stepping closer to Billowtail. "Very special indeed."

All the other squirrels had gathered around again, with question in their eyes.

"Please, take it." She pushed the pinecone into Billowtail's paws. "You will all need strength for the journey."

"Thank you for your abundant kindness," said Sugarcoat, with a slight bow of the head. She wrapped her arms around the pinecone to relieve Billowtail of the heavy load.

"No," said Billowtail, taking the pinecone back

and returning it to the stranger. "We cannot accept this. We have taken far too much from you already. We beg your apologies for our selfishness."

"Selfishness? How could anyone like you use that term to describe yourself? I have lived a full nine years and never once in that time have I met one squirrel who would do what you are doing. And today I have met five. Yes, oh, yes. I consider this a very special occasion indeed!"

"Well then, you make the first tear!" Sugarcoat insisted, referring to the method squirrels use of tearing off the bark of pinecones to get to the nuts underneath.

"Well, look at us," Sir Sniff declared. "We are about to tear pinecone together and we have not even introduced ourselves. I am Sir Sniff, and this is Sugarcoat, Billowtail, Nip and Tippy."

"It's a pleasure," the stranger said. "A real pleasure. And I am Lady Flora."

During the course of their dining together, Lady Flora ate very little, though the other squirrels continued to push food in front of her, especially when they found a particularly large pine nut. She ate a morsel here and there to be polite, but they all sensed she truly wished for them to take all the nourishment they could.

"I sure hope you find that little squirrel," Lady Flora said. "I'm sure his Momma is beside herself. I know I would be."

"Do you have children?" Nip asked.

"I'm afraid not," Flora said with a sadness moving over her face. "Only in my heart. I've got one there, and there he will always remain."

"You mean he's already left the drey?"

"Left the drey?" she said, absently. "No. Not, not exactly like that. No."

Tippy continued to feast on his acorn. The others stopped chewing and exchanged glances, realizing some kind of cloud had just moved in. Suddenly, Tippy noticed something had changed and he too quit munching. "What?" he asked, looking around at his friends. "What did I miss? Did I miss something?"

Sugarcoat put her finger to her lips and cast Tippy a discreet glare to silence him.

"Many seasons had passed me by." Lady Flora looked out into the sky as she spoke. "I was never given offspring. And then one day, I was granted the gift of motherhood."

The squirrels sat in silence, waiting for the rest of the story, but afraid to hear it.

"I didn't know, of course, as I prepared for the arrival of young for forty-three sunsets, how many I carried within me. But I was grateful on the day of delivery, that I had been given even this one. A beautiful little boy. I named him Hazelharp. The day of birth was well before the vernal equinox, and it had been a harsh winter, and we were surely headed for another cold snap. I didn't want to turn SliceWind out of the nest, but it's what every female does after the babies are born. Sad as it is, and you know this, Sugarcoat, we females can never fully trust our mates. There have been too many who consider children a burden and would rather dispose of them. So, I evicted him, only to have him return when the cold spell hit. He barged in and informed me he was staying with us. I put up my best and loudest arguments, but he refused to leave. A clamorous chatter ensued, which I am sure all the neighbors heard, and then a full-blown fight. There was pushing and shoving and then some clawing and finally an all-out brawl. Hazelharp just lay sleeping peacefully through it all, still blind and deaf. Still had his ears pasted down.

SliceWind's willingness to attack me for the nest was further confirmation that my instincts were correct, and I could not allow him near the baby. Looking back on it, I should have just taken my son and left and found a new drey. But a pinky would have surely died without warm shelter, and I had not prepared well. Maybe because I had been disappointed for so many litter-less years, I had not bothered to build a second drey that year, like good mama squirrels do in the event their original home becomes infested with mites or fleas. And my baby paid the ultimate price for my failure."

A cool wind swept through the trees, reaching down to the ground, causing Billowtail a slight shiver.

"I told him I have Hazelharp to think about," Flora continued. "And then his eyes flashed and I saw something rabid in them."

"Something rabid? What do you mean?" Nip asked with wide eyes.

"Maybe I should say *evil*," she said.

Although squirrels are far from perfect wherever you're from, no one in The Alliance had ever known an evil squirrel.

"Little Hazelharp had just stirred a tiny bit and caught SliceWind's attention. He stormed over and grabbed him and said, 'I can see you are concerned for this one, that he won't have a nice warm nest. Well let's just make sure you don't have that to worry about anymore.' Hazelharp was screaming and squealing and crying and I rushed to him and SliceWind held him up over his head, where I couldn't reach him. I tried. I tried so hard, but I couldn't. And then, he—I still can't believe it. I can't believe he did it."

Tippy and Nip fixed their eyes on Flora. Billowtail, Sugarcoat and Sir Sniff looked down at their paws or their bellies or their feet, waiting, fearful of what they were going to hear.

"He hurled Hazelharp out of the nest onto the hard ground thirty feet below."

Other than her sniffing, Flora was quiet for some time, as was everyone else. They had all ceased eating and stared down at their food. It might have been the first time in the history of the world that a squirrel was not interested in a nut.

"It will be in Hazelharp's honor, then, and in preservation of his memory, that we will bring back Puttermunch," Sir Sniff announced valiantly. "As sure as tree roots are deep and chipmunks are shallow, we will find him. And we will henceforth be known as The Hazelharp Alliance. Miss Squig will be happy to know that *we* have a name"

"I just don't understand," Flora said. "How did Mrs. Poggins find five squirrels who would care about her baby?"

"The world seems very cruel to you, Lady Flora, I know," said Sir Sniff. "And it is understandable. But there is good too. I cannot tell you I have come all this way for the sake of a pinky. But I have come for the sake of all that is good and right and just."

"Well, uh, Nip and I, we were just looking for adventure," Tippy said. "And it has been awesome!"

"And we felt kind of bad for Mrs. Poggins," Nip added. "She has been so kind to us."

"Well, I would rather not be here," said Sugarcoat. "I am here because I have been given a great responsibility. I possess something valuable and I cannot hoard it and keep it from serving others."

Billowtail wasn't sure why exactly he was there. He had always assumed it was to look for Puttermunch. In fact, up until that moment, he thought that's why they were all there.

"And what about you, Billowtail?" Lady Flora asked. "You have remained quiet."

"I don't know," said Billowtail. "Maybe I am looking for the squirrel I used to be. I too was pushed from the nest when I was a tiny pinky. I know what it feels like."

Billowtail immediately regretted having said that much. He knew there would be follow-up questions. He was not ready to hear himself tell the rest of the story.

CHAPTER FIVE

THE HAZELHARP ALLIANCE

HOW DID IT HAPPEN?" asked Lady Flora. "How did Puttermunch fall?"

Billowtail was relieved to hear that particular question and decided to be the one to answer. And this is the account he gave:

The peaceful mid-day stillness of the forest was shattered by the nauseating sound of Mrs. Poggins' screeching, followed by her wailing and finally a prolonged weeping.

She had tried to keep pace with the horse, which carried the saddlebag that Puttermunch had fallen into, but the faster she ran, the more the boy spurred his horse. He was spooked by the crazed squirrel pursuing him. He had feared squirrels ever since he was a little boy. And mice and other rodents too. Which is why he owned a cat. That, and they are soft to pet.

Finally, he'd had enough, and he grabbed his

bow from the cart behind him and shot a number of arrows at Mrs. Poggins, who jumped over two and dodged left of another, tripping over a rock and rolling into a ditch. The cart receded from view as Mrs. Poggins struggled to get up. She realized there was no way she could catch up, and she had left Puttermunch's brothers and sisters unattended in the drey.

"There, there," Sir Sniff coaxed, taking her around the shoulder when he saw her return limping, in tears. "Why don't you start from the beginning and tell us what happened."

"Didn't anybody hear the commotion? Why did nobody come to my aid? Puttermunch! My little Puttermunch. He's fallen and they've taken him. Please, Sir Sniff, you must go after him!"

"Me? Well, I am much too—"

"Please, you've got to try to do something. Please! My ankle is no good now. Plus, I have the rest of my pinkies who need their mother's milk."

"But I fear I am no match for a galloping horse, Mrs. Poggins. Not anymore, anyway."

"Oh, my Puttermunch," she wailed.

"Oh very well, very well. Which way did you say he went?"

"I will go," said Billowtail, peeking out from behind a tree. He had witnessed the whole thing, but frozen in fear at the sight of the human.

Sir Sniff nodded and winked his approval. "You just look after the rest of your pinkies," he said to Mrs. Poggins, walking her back to her tree. "Billowtail and I will take care of this."

"And me!" declared Tippy, who stuck his head up through a woodpecker hole in a hollow log, lying at the foot of Mrs. Poggins' tree.

"And how do you propose to get at Puttermunch with that Great Pinky in the way?" came the question from up in the neighboring tree.

"We will strategize." Sir Sniff craned his neck and answered instinctively without worrying too much about who he was answering. "We will find a way."

"I will accompany you and help you strategize," said Sugarcoat.

"Please, please go quickly," begged Mrs. Poggins, breathlessly, behind her tears.

"Wait! Wait! Wait!" Miss Squig had popped her head out of a hole. The middle-aged ground squirrel lifted her body out nimbly and scurried to grab Sir Sniff's arm. "The boy is very far ahead by now. You will have no indication of his location or which way he is heading." Miss Squig put her hands on Sugarcoat's shoulders and peered into her eyes. "There is something that must be bestowed on you," she said. "Come."

"What is it?" asked Sugarcoat impatiently. "We must not waste time. Puttermunch is getting farther and farther away from us."

"It will only take a minute and it will be well worth your time." The sleek animal disappeared into a hole in the ground, and Sugarcoat, hesitating for a few seconds, followed. It was uncommon for a tree squirrel to go underground, and it must have felt as odd to Sugarcoat as it looked to the others, who were impatient to start their quest, understanding it was going to get harder and harder the longer they waited.

It wasn't a minute before Miss Squig came back up without Sugarcoat.

"Where is she?" asked Billowtail. "Where is Sugarcoat?"

"She will be up momentarily," replied the ground squirrel. "Now, let's see. What will you call yourselves?"

"What do you mean?" asked Billowtail. "We are Billowtail, Tippy and Sir Sniff. And Sugarcoat.

Of course."

"And Nip," injected a squirrel who had seemed to pop out of nowhere. "I am coming along too."

"No, Billowtail," said Miss Squig. "Billowtail is who *you* are. That's not a *we*. That's an *I*."

"We?" asked Billowtail.

"We?" puzzled Tippy.

"Are we a *we*?" Nip asked.

"The instant you set your feet on the path before you, you will be a *we*." Miss Squig explained.

"Wow," said Nip, looking questioningly at Tippy. "I've never been in a *we* before."

"Is that kind of like an *us*?" Sir Sniff asked.

"Very much so," said Miss Squig.

"I don't know about this," said Nip.

"What if we can't do it?" asked Tippy.

"We are tree squirrels," Billowtail said to Miss Squig. "We aren't like you."

"You must learn it," Miss Squig said. "There will come a moment when everything will depend on it. You tree squirrels have always looked down on us ground dwellers—"

"No, I didn't mean it like that," Billowtail said.

Miss Squig put her paw up. "You assume we are weak because we cannot do everything on our own. We need each other. Our very survival depends on the other. But you will see. There is great wisdom in our design."

"So," said Sir Sniff looking from one squirrel to the next. "What shall *we* call ourselves?"

There was a long silence. Billowtail looked at his foot, which was waggling nervously. Tippy cleaned his tail while chewing on a nutshell fragment that had finally come loose after days of being embedded in his inner cheek. Sir Sniff gazed at the ground and rubbed his chin thoughtfully.

Nip looked up into the sky, with soft pensive eyes, as if he were watching the slow descent of the world's most beautiful idea. "How about Fluffy?" he offered.

"Fluffy?" Miss Squig scoffed. "No, no, no, no, no. I think you've missed the point."

"What's wrong with the name Fluffy? If I ever have a son—"

"Yes, Nip," said Sir Sniff. "Fluffy may very well be a fine name for an individual squirrel. We are trying to come up with a name for a group of squirrels. Just one name for the entire bunch of us."

"Well we can't all be named Fluffy," Nip said. "That would be very confusing. And rather dull."

Miss Squig rolled her eyes up and back into her skull and slapped her forehead. "Look," she said, "For example, when we were forced to migrate to new territory four seasons ago, we called ourselves the Swiftails. See, we all still kept our names, so I remained Miss Squig and Flickertail remained Flickertail and Loulou remained Loulou, et cetera, et cetera, et cetera. But together we shared yet another name."

"Oh, I get it!" Nip exclaimed. "We can be called *The Fluffies*!"

Tippy and Billowtail looked at each other, trying to contain their smiles. Miss Squig and Sir Sniff shook their heads at each other.

"Oh, for Pete's sake," said Miss Squig. "When you come up with a name for your alliance, let me know. Meanwhile, I'm just going to call you *The Alliance*.

"What does Alliance mean?" asked Tippy.

Billowtail had wanted to know the same thing, but he didn't want to appear daft, so he didn't ask.

"It means something is about to change you in irreversible ways," Miss Squig said. "You will never be the same."

Sugarcoat emerged with her pure white coat a little less white than before.

"What happened in there?" asked Tippy.

"What did they give you?" Nip inquired.

"They did not *give* me anything." Sugarcoat looked a little dazed.

"What's that on your tail?" asked Sir Sniff taking a step toward her.

"Don't touch it!" said Sugarcoat twisting to grab her tail and hugging it to herself. "Let's go. Time is wasting."

"But what is it?" asked Nip.

"It looks like you have a very thick strand of spider silk wrapped around your tail," said Tippy.

"It's called a thread, actually. And I don't know much about it. Where's Billowtail? We have to move out."

Sir Sniff pointed with a look of annoyance. Billowtail had dug up a number of his nuts and was taking instructions from Sheilagwen the chipmunk on how to stretch his cheeks to pack in as much food as possible.

"Leave it all here," Sir Sniff advised. "We will get food along the way."

"How do you know there is food?" Billowtail could hardly form the words since he had so much stuffed into his mouth, his lips could scarcely touch.

"I do not know how I know," Sir Sniff said in the noble tone that was so natural to him. "I just know. Now let us go."

CHAPTER SIX

CROSSING BRIDGES

YET ANOTHER RIVER and yet another bridge. At least a bridge tends to break up the monotony of the road. Billowtail liked to walk atop the low railing, which provided just enough room for his passage, but would not have allowed for two-way traffic, had another squirrel come by the other way.

The Alliance was crossing this bridge because Sugarcoat caught the tail end of a conversation at the fair in Pamplona, after the satisfying feast with Lady Flora. A traveler had just come from across the bridge in Puente la Reina and had seen a mother cat nursing a baby squirrel. The Alliance set out with new hope.

The stone bridge was a series of arches that started small and grew larger as they reached the middle of the river, making for a slight uphill climb toward the center and then a gradual descent into the next village. Billowtail found himself fascinated by the growing and then diminishing size of the arches as he tipped his head sideways over the edge to watch bridge and water come together and turn arch into circle by way of reflection.

Tippy jumped up behind him and followed closely. And then Nip behind Tippy. Sugarcoat, scampering with Sir Sniff in the shadow where the low-wall meets the bridge's footpath, sent up a motherly warning about staying away from the edge.

"Yes, Sugarcoat," Tippy said, making sure his tone revealed how tiresome her nagging had become. "We'll be careful."

"Sugarcoat is just trying to keep us safe, Tippy," said Billowtail. "We ought to listen to her."

"I'm listening," Tippy said, making a high-speed pass on Billowtail's left. "I always listen."

"Would that it were true," said the eldest squirrel. Sir Sniff was nearing the last third of his life, so his prime was well behind him. He was getting a bit soft around the middle and couldn't scamper as fast as he once did, but his endurance was uncanny. The Alliance had not had to stop even once to give him a rest. In fact, it was he who was often the inspiration for covering ground. "Press on," he would say, in his steady tone.

"Look what I see over there, at the end of the bridge!" Tippy exclaimed. "Dogwood!"

He was flying now, not watching his feet or the bridge or anything else, really, except for the flaming orange-yellow blaze of leaves ahead of him, amongst which, he was sure, there would be luscious berries dangling. He hadn't had dogberries since last fall. The tree back home was not bearing fruit quite yet when he left. Dogberries were his favorite dessert, but more important than that, they reminded him of home.

"Tippy! Slow down!" Sugarcoat commanded.

Just as Billowtail was about to issue his own warning at Tippy, the young squirrel's toe snagged a jagged stone, and he toppled head over tail straight down the middle of the rail, landing spread eagle.

"Tippy!" exclaimed Billowtail and Sniff at once.

"Be careful!" barked Sugarcoat.

Billowtail noticed that females always seem to come up with this directive after someone falls or bumps their head or sprains their ankle or eats the rotten plum. What exactly does being careful do to undo what's already been done?

Billowtail helped Tippy to his feet. Nip just stared, dumbfounded, unable to materialize any worthy adjectives. "Whoa," he said, breathlessly.

"I'm fine, I'm fine," Tippy reassured everyone as Sugarcoat fussed at him, and Sniff offered a moral that could be learned from the mishap: "You failed to follow the advice of wisdom. This makes you very foolish indeed. Your actions could have had catastrophic consequences. It is only good fortune that has saved you. You might not be so fortunate the next time."

No sooner was Tippy up on his feet than he was off running again, and no sooner was he running than he was tumbling again, this time not in a straight line, but in a clumsy and hazardous jumble that inspired a terrified and united gasp from all four of Tippy's companions. And then, he rolled right off the edge.

Before they could comprehend the unthinkable reality of what their eyes had revealed, Billowtail let out a horrifying scream: "No!!!!! Tippy!!! No!!!!" He flung himself belly first onto the low wall and hung his head over the edge, expecting to see an expanding circular ripple in the water below. But there was no water below. It was solid land. The squirrels had gotten far enough over the bridge that they were now directly over the river-bank and not the water. Billowtail had, of course, not noticed it before, but the builders of the bridge had installed, across its entirety on the outer edge, a very narrow ledge, designed either for decorative purposes or for the passage of baby field mice. And that is where Tippy hung by his sharp claws, his tail swaying wildly, his feet swinging and legs flailing, unable to make contact with anything but air. Without a solid perch for his feet, Tippy had no hope of making the vertical ascent back up to the top of the bridge. He had only two choices: hang on and continue to flail, or let go.

Now, if Tippy had been another type of animal, his predicament might not have been so dire. Had he been a member of a species that understands teamwork, there might have been some hope for him. Wolves work together with their pack mates to bring down a caribou. Meerkats organize day care for the members who have to leave their young to go out and hunt. Bees collaborate to build hives and serve their queen. But squirrels? They do one thing for one squirrel. They gather nuts for themselves. Outside of a mother squirrel's love for her young, squirrels are on their own. It's not that they don't care about their fellow squirrel. They are just not equipped with the skills to work together. If they were, this is how Tippy might have been saved:

Billowtail would have slung himself over the edge of the railing, hanging tight with all his might to the rough stone of the wall. Nip would have climbed down Billowtail's back and grabbed onto his tail. Sir Sniff would have climbed down Billowtail and then down Nip, to grab onto Nip's tail. And finally, Sugarcoat would have formed the lowest part of the squirrel chain, letting herself go limp so her tail would be just in reach of Tippy, who would stretch with one hand with all his might and grab, sinking his paw into the fur, until it found the more reliable bone to latch onto. Then, he would have hoisted himself up over all the squirrel bodies to the very top, climbing back onto the bridge, panting with relief. Then Sugarcoat would have gone next, climbing up over the squirrels to join Tippy at the top. Then Sir Sniff and then Nip, who would turn and give Billowtail his paw and pull him up onto the bridge. And then they would all be safe.

But squirrels do not operate that way. They do not think that way. So, it looked like Tippy was going to have to perish. His strength to hold on was quickly giving way, and he probably had seconds and not minutes until he plummeted. If he were anywhere else on the bridge, he might have stood a chance, since squirrels do doggy paddle, using their tails as a rudder, though they prefer dry land because swimming is quite a strenuous activity for them and they don't get much practice from their usual position in treetops. All of this was a moot point, however, since they were over land and not water. Squirrel tails can be used as parachutes for short-distance falls, but a fall from this height would probably mean either sudden death or a spinal cord injury and then a slow, agonizing death. Sugarcoat barked impossible directions at Tippy as his body swayed and dangled, appearing to blow in the wind, which was impossible since there was not the slightest disturbance in the weather.

"Hoist your leg up against the wall and use it for leverage," she called down.

"Don't let go, Tippy," Sir Sniff commanded, laying belly-down on the low wall, his head hanging over the edge. "You're OK as long as you keep hanging on. Just hang on."

Tippy had only one thought: how much he wanted a hug from his mother. He used to think of her when he woke up cold and frightened from a dream. He would imagine her hugging him, and he would feel safe and warm again and fall back to sleep. Now he was thinking how devastated she would be when she learned the news that he had fallen to his death. That thought kept his fingernails attached to the grainy rock. Meanwhile, Nip and Billowtail scurried frantically in circles, chirping and twitching their tails. They, themselves, weren't even sure what kind of help this would be, but they didn't know what else to do. As it turned out, it helped quite a bit. The commotion caught the attention of a Great Pinky who was just beginning to cross the bridge, and hastened his pace in order to see what had the little creatures in such distress. Upon seeing Tippy dangling, the man straddled the wall, hoisting one foot far enough over to get it under Tippy's rear end and gave the panicked squirrel a ride on his sandal and a boost up over the wall. Billowtail had seen this man before, he was sure. Tippy grabbed onto the man's waist rope and pulled himself up inch by inch, using the coarseness of the man's brown robe for traction against his long toenails. The man placed his hand beside Tippy, who hopped on and received a ride right up to his face. Billowtail could see the man's wide-stretched lips under his beard. Sugarcoat had told the squirrels that Great Pinkies call that a smile, and they do it to show delight and sometimes love. You might even say it is a highly-prized treasure. Billowtail wished he could manage one of those. Just watching someone else do it caused a happy feeling to wash over him, and he was certain the feeling would last much longer if he could participate in it himself. All fear had left him and he scurried closer to get a better look into the man's face. Now, he knew. This was the man who saved him from the dog.

It is difficult for squirrels to remember faces. They never pay too much attention to even the faces of other squirrels. It just isn't important to remember what anybody looks like. But this face –

the face of the man who saved squirrels (at least on two occasions) – was to be remembered. Billowtail felt as if their paths would cross again. It was a strange feeling, a bit disconcerting actually. Squirrels are not known to have premonitions. Other than knowing the winter will be cold, the spring will bring fresh food and litters, squirrels don't know much about the future, though they spend a great deal of time thinking about it. They are, indeed, excellent planners. They seem to share this trait with the Great Pinkies. Bridges, of course, are a testament to this fact. The existence of a bridge signifies that someone has planned for someone to cross it, just as the existence of a buried nut signifies that someone plans to dine.

It seems, though, that the similarities between the two species might stop there. Dramatic differences exist between them. For one thing, as it relates to food, sometimes squirrels forget where they put their nuts. Actually, more than sometimes. But they would never purposely leave a nut uneaten. Yet, on more than one occasion of this journey, Sugarcoat had heard of a Great Pinky choosing not to eat food. They referred to it as a "fast." Sugarcoat could not tell her comrades exactly what that meant as she had not heard a full discussion on the matter. All she could gather is that one chooses not to eat out of love for someone who suffered a horrific, torturous death to save you. Like The Alliance, the humans too, are looking for someone. But unlike The Alliance, the Great Pinkies seem to be searching for someone already dead, perhaps even the person they are fasting for. Apparently, even the bridge that proved to be almost fatal to Tippy was constructed to help the humans find the one they are looking for. Dona Mayor, wife of King Sancho III, had the bridge built for this type of Great Pinky they call "pilgrim."

The town then became known as "Queen's

Bridge." Apparently, the pilgrims will need to pass over the bridge and through the town and cross many other bridges and pass through many other towns to reach a place called Santiago de Compostela, where the body of a great, great Great Pinky named St. James rests. At least that's what Sugarcoat thought she overheard.

It is quite a puzzle. The squirrels felt a sort of pity for the humans, who must be terribly desperate to spend so much time searching for someone already dead. The squirrels were not deceiving themselves. There was, of course, a real chance the one they were searching for would be dead by the time they found him, or for that matter, may have already been dead, as any passing day can usher in the demise of a fragile baby squirrel, especially one away from its mother. But there was also a real chance—a good chance, the squirrels liked to think—that Puttermunch would survive. And this is what sets the squirrels apart from the humans in their logic. It makes no sense to search for one you know is already dead, no matter how good or loved he might be. Puttermunch is surely loved, but if the squirrels knew with certainty that he was dead, they would shed some tears, pay respects and go home and continue to build up their stores of nuts.

Unfortunately, Puente la Reina provided no opportunity to verify Puttermunch's survival, as the boy was with his cart constantly, and the cat never emerged from under the blankets. So, it was onto the next town, which they all hoped could be reached in some way other than crossing a bridge.

CHAPTER SEVEN

LEAF TUBE MELODIES

THE NEXT STRETCH OF ROAD brought new layers of blisters and higher levels of dread. A rest in a meadow couldn't have been more welcome.

"The boy is going to climb Peña Bajenza," Sugarcoat announced as the squirrels dined on dandelions and daisies.

"What is that?" asked Billowtail, wrestling with a long white pedal, which was putting up a valiant fight to keep itself from being stuffed headlong into a very determined squirrel's mouth.

"We've been looking at it for quite some time now," Sugarcoat said.

"That big rock over there?" Nip asked.

"Yes, that big rock."

"How can anyone climb that?" Billowtail asked. "That has to be the height of thirty trees, but with no branches to grab onto."

"Why is he going to the top?" Sir Sniff asked. "Is he looking for something?"

"Yes, he is looking for a view."

"A view?" said Nip. "What is that?"

"Apparently, humans like to climb things to look down at the things below."

"Wouldn't they see things better if they just looked at things from where the things actually are?" Billowtail asked.

"And there's a little bit of bad news too," said Sugarcoat, ignoring the question which had so obvious an answer.

"You mean in addition to having to climb a gigantic rock just to look at stuff down below?" asked Billowtail.

"Yes. In addition to that."

"Well, what is it?" Nip asked.

"That big rock is home to a colony of vultures. They are known as Pharaoh's chickens. The boy has some kind of fascination with the species and is taking a detour to try to spot them."

"Should we not wait here for him?" Billowtail suggested. They were on safe and soft ground, strewn with an abundance of wildflowers and large swatches of grass tall enough to hide squirrels.

"No, we can't," said Sugarcoat. "We have to follow him. He is on a journey and therefore it is not likely he will come back to the same place he left."

"What an unfortunate name," said Sir Sniff. "Pharaoh's chickens. So undignified."

"To belong to a Pharaoh doesn't sound so shabby to me," said Tippy.

"But a chicken?" said Nip. "I don't care whose chicken you are. That's just brutal to the self esteem."

"Brutal is what those chickens are going to do to us," said Billowtail.

"No worries," said Tippy. "Vultures eat dead animals right? And we're not dead." There was an abundance of optimism in his voice, as usual. "So, there you go." He said this happily, as if not being dead had its only true advantage in the fact that the vultures would not prefer to eat you.

"Well, vultures may prefer to have their food killed for them, but they're not too picky when they're hungry," said Sugarcoat. "If they see a small animal, they will eat it whether it's dead yet or not."

"Well, we don't have to worry if small animals are all they are after," Tippy said.

"Tippy, I don't know how to break this to you," said Sir Sniff, "but we are small animals."

"Small? Really Sir, meaning no disrespect, but how can you say that? We are quite large compared to many."

"Such as?" Sugarcoat asked.

"Grasshoppers."

"And the grasshoppers are large compared to ants," said Sugarcoat. "But you compared to a vulture—"

"Ho—ho—hold on there, with all due respect, Sugarcoat," said Tippy. "I prefer to view myself in relation to grasshoppers. Or even ants."

Billowtail had retreated to a tall tree branch and was trying to ignore as much of the conversation below as was possible. The talk of birds of prey threatened to conjure a past that would torment and paralyze him and render him useless to the mission.

"Billowtail," Sir Sniff hollered up into the tree. "We're moving out."

Billowtail climbed down slowly as his comrades took their last bites and scurried into a bush adjacent to where the boy was packing up his belongings.

"Sir Sniff," Billowtail said. "It appears the boy will indeed be making a round trip. He has not hitched his horse to the cart."

"Oh, he will hitch him," Sir Sniff said. "He would not leave his possessions behind."

Billowtail knew that to be true, but he was employing wishful thinking. It was the only hopeful thought he could muster at the moment. "Well, you never know," Billowtail said. "It seems a very uncertain route for a horse and cart. Maybe even treacherous."

"Others have gone before," Sugarcoat assured him.

They all watched as the boy untied his horse from a tree and led him to the cart.

"Well, I guess that settles it," Sir Sniff said.

Billowtail's heart sank. "I think you will all have to go on without me," he said.

"What?" Sugarcoat exclaimed. "What are you talking about?"

"I can't go up there," Billowtail said, his mouth sticky and dry. "I think this is the end of the journey for me. I am of no use to The Alliance. I will return to Bon Arbre."

"No," Sugarcoat said, emphatically. "You will not return to Bon Arbre. This is not an option."

"We are all soft and cowardly and unaccustomed to hardship," Sir Sniff said. "That must change. It will change."

"What do you mean we?" said Tippy indignantly. "Do you mean to say that I have never experienced any hardships? Bon Arbre is full of hardships. I cannot tell you how many times I have been poked in the eye by a pine needle. Gives me a sore, scratchy eye for two days or more. Tears up real bad in the middle of the day when the sun is brightest. And what about all the times I have been poked in the interior jaw by a nutshell? Gets lodged the wrong way and the soft tissue in the mouth stays irritated for hours."

"Tippy," Sir Sniff said, "if we're going to be honest, we will all agree that nothing back home could have toughened us up enough for what lies ahead. Neither a pine needle to the eye nor nutshell to the jaw will come close."

"Well, I'm with Billowtail," Nip said. "I am going back home with him."

Billowtail had a sudden thought of his mother, of her bravery and her steel. And her love for her children. "No, Nip," he said. "We promised Mrs. Poggins. I'm not going home until we find Puttermunch. Look. The boy's got his horse all hitched up now. Let's go."

If birds of prey were going to swoop from the sky and take him, Billowtail reasoned, at least he would die doing the same thing his mother died doing – trying to save the life of a young squirrel.

"OK," said Nip. "I'll press on. But don't you think it unwise to have Tippy in high places?"

"Huh?" Tippy said, pulling his head out of a hole he had found under a bush, a possible nut stash belonging to another squirrel. "What did I miss?"

"We'll keep him away from the ledges," said Sir Sniff. "Now come on. The boy is leaving."

There was little cover on the big bald red rock the boy chose to climb, and as the vultures circled overhead, Billowtail became increasingly annoyed at the boy for having chosen it for pure recreational purposes and for beholding some sort of beauty he had not seen before. It was unnecessary to his destination, whatever that was. The squirrels had to stay a good distance behind the boy, since there was little vegetation to hide in for much of the trip. Billowtail felt a panic as the vultures circled over some poor dead animal just paces from the path. None of the squirrels could determine what kind of animal it was. Billowtail supposed he should be grateful the vultures were busy. He felt a bit guilty for having thought that way, but since the animal was already dead, he reasoned, it was better for the vultures to be feasting there than creating any new death.

It became clearer as the squirrels walked on that they were not going to get up and down the mountain before nightfall. They would be spending the night with the vultures. Billowtail resolved to stay awake all night, hoping his exhaustion would allow it. He once tried to wait up for his aunt, and he didn't even make it half the night. The guilt of falling asleep never had gone away. When his aunt Posey did not come home, everyone theorized she was eaten. She wasn't very fast and not at all nimble in her later years. Billowtail never could get over the fact that he was enjoying a sound and peaceful sleep while she was in her death agony. He was never particularly close to his aunt, and he was ashamed of his own lack of devastation at her loss. If he could have done anything to bring her back, he would have. Not because he missed her, but because it would have alleviated his guilt.

The group reached the top of the rock just as the sun was setting. The boy looked off the mountain, onto the view below. Then he turned and looked the other way.

The squirrels had found a cluster of rocks to hide behind. The absence of full sun created the type of cold that seemed to stand right on top the mountain and seep into whatever was standing with it. In this case, it was Billowtail's bones. He made a 360-degree scan and saw nothing but sky.

"Are they n—n—nocturnal?" he shivered.

"Who?" Sugarcoat asked.

"V—V—Vultures."

"I do not think so," she said.

Billowtail issued a sigh of relief that chattered his teeth.

"But I cannot be sure," she continued. "The only raptors I know who hunt at night are owls.

But then again, I had never heard of a Pharaoh's chicken twenty-four hours ago, so I have no idea what their sleep habits might be."

"I sure hope that mother cat knows what she's doing," Nip said. "Otherwise, her litter and little Puttermunch are going to be in serious danger."

"I am staying awake to guard them, uh, I mean him," said Billowtail.

"Great," said Sir Sniff, "and I will stand watch over The Alliance. The rest of you can get some sleep."

Billowtail was about to offer that one squirrel could watch both the cart and The Alliance. But he suspected Sir Sniff did not trust him to stay awake. That was alright with him, because he did not trust himself either. And he was happy for the company.

Birds of prey were Billowtail's biggest fear, even in front of famine. Most squirrels would not agree. Starving to death, is a long, slow, painful process. But it was not hunger that took his mother from him.

There was a bit of travelling light left, and Billowtail was grateful that the boy moved on from that vast openness to a stand of pines, choosing it as his camp site, after having traversed leagues of naked red rock and areas of low-lying shrubs and trees that could barely be called trees – more like large bushes themselves. His relief dissipated when he saw the colony of vultures roosting on a dead pine, but he hung onto Sugarcoat's belief that they would sleep at night.

The squirrels chose a tall tree, as far away as possible from the vultures, but not too far away from the boy, and filled themselves on pine nuts before drifting off to sleep in the branches. The smell of pine provided some comfort to Billowtail, and the nearly full moon helped keep him awake. The vultures, indeed, were all still, silhouetted against the round moon. Billowtail had never, in his adult life, seen anything so hideous. Two dozen or more raptors, spiky-headed and cold-hearted, standing still as stones in a spindly tree, on a lonely mountain.

Sir Sniff and Billowtail sat back to back on a branch low enough to get down the tree if need be and high enough to remove themselves from some of the dangers, whatever they may be. Billowtail had a clear line of sight of the cart, and Sir Sniff watched over Sugarcoat, Tippy and Nip who had fallen asleep three branches below.

"Hmmfgh," grunted Sir Sniff. "I didn't know Tippy snored so loud."

Billowtail smiled. "You ought to hear yourself. Sir Sniff. Sir."

The elder squirrel's face broke into a smile, and they both suppressed a long chuckle. Being quiet and still while awake is difficult for squirrels, at least for any extended period of time.

"Sir Sniff, why do you think we are here?"

"We are following the boy. It is our way to Puttermunch."

"But why specifically us?"

"I don't know, Billowtail. I am not sure anyone can answer that, even if they understood the question."

Sir Sniff yawned, and then Billowtail yawned. He had been resisting that urge for quite some time because he knew what typically followed yawns. But since even Sir Sniff allowed himself one, Billowtail indulged.

"What did you mean back there, Billowtail," Sir Sniff said in a soft voice. "About falling from the nest?"

"It was my own fault," Billowtail sighed. "I was so anxious to see what was outside the nest. My Momma warned me to stay away from the edge. But my curiosity got the best of me one day when she was out foraging. I had to look out. My brother and sister also wanted to see, so they squeezed in next to me to look, and we were all enjoying the idea of one day exploring what was out there. We were all being less than careful and a little rambunctious, making up great adventures and then speaking them into each other's minds. And then in our frenzied merriment, I felt something press against my back, and I lost my footing and fell to the ground, landing unharmed in a pile of leaves."

"Thank heavens you survived the fall."

"Yes. I survived. But that fall cost my mother her life."

"How, son? How did she die?"

"I—I don't want to say it, Sir Sniff. It is too awful to say."

"I understand, kid," he said, patting Billowtail on the shoulder. "I understand."

"Have you had things happen to you that are too awful to say?"

"Indeed, kid. I think we all have."

"Then, you do understand."

"I do," he yawned and stretched. "Hey, if I can find you a proper instrument, would you be able to play a tune? Might help keep us awake."

"I don't know," said Billowtail. "I doubt there is a reed around here that would be of any use. Plus I have not played in so long."

"I will be right back" said Sir Sniff, scurrying down the tree.

"Wait, Sir Sniff," said Billowtail. "Don't bother trying—"

"I'll only be a minute, Billowtail. It will be OK."

Billowtail decided to watch the vultures, since he couldn't watch both the cart and the slumbering squirrels. The horrid creatures remained motionless against the black sky, and since the picture he was looking at didn't change, it was dull enough to make his eyelids fall. He jerked himself awake, and turned his body to look at his friends, then at the cart below. Sugarcoat was right. These beastly birds were not budging until morning, you could bet on that. A little cat nap until Sir Sniff returned wouldn't hurt. He let everything go dark.

It was a "whoosh" that startled him from his sleep, and he blinked hard as his heart pounded in his throat. The first thing he saw was the vulture tree, and it hadn't changed at all. Maybe he had dreamed the whoosh. He tried to settle himself, as he heard his own heart pounding in his ears. He wanted to call for Sir Sniff, but he didn't dare make a sound. Sugarcoat, Nip and Tippy were still fast asleep. The boy was still sleeping on the ground next to his cart, and the blanket was still covering the bed of the wagon. Billowtail looked up into the night sky and saw nothing but the tops of pine trees all around. And then it dawned on him. An owl! He was so focused on vultures, he had forgotten to be afraid of owls! This would certainly be the time of night for them to hunt. What if an owl had gotten Sir Sniff? Why had Sir Sniff been gone so long? How long, exactly, had he been gone? There was no way for Billowtail to know how long he had been asleep. Was it just a few seconds? Or was it an hour? Oh, why did he let himself sleep?

Then, he remembered. Owl wings make no noise. The whoosh must have belonged to someone else. Or to his own imagination. He turned his head to look behind him, and something so shocking was headed for him, he inhaled an unexpected gasp, sucking so much saliva down his windpipe, he entered an uncontrollable coughing fit. The creature swooped in and landed right next to him on the branch. Billowtail shielded his head with his arm as he tried to stifle his cough.

"You OK there, mate?"

Billowtail slowly removed his arm from one eye, then the other. "What on earth?!!!" he said under his breath. It was a squirrel!

"Hello," said the stranger. "You OK?"

"Wow," said Billowtail. "How did you do that?"

"Do what?"

"Fly!"

"Oh, I don't really fly. It's called gliding. Looks fancy, like flying, doesn't it? It's all in the armpit flaps here," he said, pulling on the skin connected at the wrists and ankles.

"Wow," was all Billowtail could manage.

"I am Pip Timbersham."

"Oh, uh, I am Billowtail. Have you seen my friend Sir Sniff?"

"Yes, he is now my friend as well. He is coming along. He has a present for you."

"A present?"

"Says you are quite the musician."

"I am? He does?"

"Yes, and I was able to put his mind at ease, and I will put yours there as well, and let you know those vultures are harmless until sunrise."

"Well, well," called a voice from the ground. "I see you found my friend Billowtail."

"Sir Sniff!" Billowtail cried. "I am sorry. I fell asleep for a minute and I–"

"Oh, yes," Sir Sniff said. "More than a minute actually. I heard the snoring. The whole mountain heard the snoring."

"Yes, well, I–"

"No harm done," Sir Sniff said climbing up the tree.

"What's that on your back?" Billowtail asked.

Sir Sniff steadied himself on the branch with Pip and Billowtail and pulled one of the two long tubular objects from a makeshift scabbard he had fashioned out of bark and twine. Pip took it and put it to his lips, blowing hard until his cheeks filled like balloons, creating a most beautiful tone. What followed was a melody, so soft and sweet, it could have drifted on the lightest clouds all the way to the heavens.

"Here," Pip said to Billowtail. "Try it."

When Billowtail took it in his hands, he realized it was a long tender green leaf, rolled lengthwise and tied with a curly string-like piece of vine that made him think of the items his mother had used to make the drey for him and his siblings.

Billowtail put the leaf tube to his lips and blew.

"You are a natural!" cried Pip, as Sir Sniff handed him the other one. "It sounds gorgeous!"

Billowtail and Pip played random melodies together, which amazingly, was never discordant and sometimes was even harmonious.

Sir Sniff sat and smiled and waved his finger in the air as if he were responsible for and in command of the glorious sound. He looked pleased and proud.

Time passed quickly, and when everything began to turn from black to gray, it was decided they should end the concert and wake the others to ready themselves for the trip down the mountain.

"Thank you for the company," Billowtail said to Pip.

"And the music," said Sir Sniff.

"It is I who thanks you," the new friend said with a slight bow. "It is rare for me to find someone gifted in music with whom I can play. Well, good morrow, mates." He stepped off the branch and soared to the next tree.

"Wait," called Billowtail. "You didn't get to meet our friends and you forgot your—"

"Keep it!" called Pip. "Can't carry it anyway. Will make a new one. Must go now, Billowtail and Sir Sniff. The daylight is not for flying squirrels. Too many birds of prey, too little natural protection. Must get to my safe haven before the monsters awake."

He leapt from the branch, extending his arms

and legs. Unfurling his flaps and turning himself into a nearly perfect square, Pip Timbersham disappeared into the dawn.

CHAPTER EIGHT

FLYING ARROWS

IF IT WASN'T FOR THE FACT that both Billow-tail and Sir Sniff had seen it, and they were not known for making things up, no one would have known whether to believe that there is such a thing as a flying squirrel. That was the topic of conversation on the way to the next destination. They had to keep their voices low, as they were travelling fairly closely behind the boy. But the wagon wheels schlepping through the mud helped drown out a great deal of noise that might be made by a band of squirrels.

Billowtail wished he could play his leaf, as he would have liked to become accomplished at walking while making music. But who knew what kind of sound it would make while wet? The rain had not let up since morning. But playing a tune might have taken Billowtail's mind off of last night. He was still perplexed about what had made that whooshing sound. He noticed when Pip left, there was nothing but a silent glide. So it couldn't have been a flying squirrel he had heard. He must have dreamed the wing noise.

The boy had made a couple of new friends who accompanied him and engaged in a steady stream of conversation. This assisted Sugarcoat in gathering intelligence. Fortunately, squirrels have a fine sense of hearing, so she could hear the boy from the far distance she had to keep to avoid being noticed.

She was able to learn that the boy was an orphan, whose mother had died of pneumonia when he was three and whose father died of typhoid eight years later. His father was a horseshoer and had taught him the trade. The boy was able to earn enough to buy some rye and barley bread and some cheese every few days by shoeing horses in villages he passed through. On the days when there was no money to buy food, the boy would take his bow and arrow and shoot whatever he would find in the woods and build a fire and roast it. Most times it was a hedgehog or a squirrel. These were the safest animals to hunt, since in some place, the land was owned by a lord, and you would get your hands cut off if you shot a boar or a deer or a hare, a punishment he surely did not deserve, though there were some days in his past when he was so hungry, he would steal. He stole some wheat bread once, the first he'd ever had on a non-Christmas day. Only the nobles could afford wheat on a regular basis since it was costly to grow, requiring special conditions.

As much as they appreciated all the information Sugarcoat was able to collect, Billowtail and the other squirrels were happy to see they were coming into another village and there would be a reprieve in the long, soppy, uneventful walk. The rain had stopped, the clouds parted and the sun went to work drying what the rain had washed. There was that pleasant feeling hanging on the still, cool air and the smell of fresh earth and greenery. The squirrels were even more pleased to see the village had food. Rows and rows of food. Rows and rows and rows and rows.

"What kind of berries are these?" said Tippy with wide eyes, as they moved past lines of short leafy bushes bearing clusters of dark fruit.

"I don't know," said Billowtail moving in to get a closer look. "I've never seen anything like these before."

The boy had parked his cart next to a small stone building and had gone inside with his new friends.

"I am going to go listen in to the Great Pinkies and see if I can determine what those berries are and if they are safe for squirrel consumption," said Sugarcoat. "Wait here."

"I'll go with you, Sugarcoat," said Sir Sniff. "Maybe it's best if none of us are alone."

Billowtail, Tippy and Nip remained, gawking at the endless rows of vine, adorned with purple orbs, glistening with drops of rain.

"Just look at them!" Tippy exclaimed. "Just look how many. I can't even see an end to them."

"They are incredible!" Nip agreed.

"Ooooh. They look so delicious," Tippy said. "I'm going to try one."

"No," Billowtail cautioned. "What if they are poisonous?"

"No, they couldn't be," Nip said. "They're too beautiful."

"And look," Tippy said. "That bird is eating one."

"What if they are poisonous to squirrels?" Billowtail said.

"Don't be silly," said Nip. "Name one thing that is poisonous to squirrels but not birds."

"Just wait until Sugarcoat and Sir Sniff get back," said Billowtail. "They're getting us information right now on what these are."

"They are obviously a very luscious fruit," Tippy said. "Tell you what. I'll be the first one to test them. If they don't kill me, they are not poisonous."

He pulled one from the vine and sunk his two front teeth into it, spewing juice that narrowly missed Billowtail's eye. Billowtail and Nip watched intently and with concern as Tippy rolled his eyes up and into the back of his head.

"Tippy," yelled Billowtail. "What is it? What's wrong?"

"Oh—my—word!" said Tippy, grabbing his chest with both paws as if a heart attack were impending. "This—this—" He licked his lips. "This is the most delicious fruit I have ever tasted." He shoved the rest of it into his mouth and chewed earnestly, with closed eyes.

"Really?" Nip planted his feet in the dirt, grasping the spherical fruit with both hands, and lay back into midair, hoping the weight of his upper body would free the fruit from the vine. It worked quite well, sending fruit and squirrel crashing into the neighboring bush.

"A most amazing treat," said Tippy, fixating on the half still in his hand and pushing muffled words out through the juicy contents of his mouth.

Nip bit into his and agreed. It was the most exquisite thing he'd ever tasted. Billowtail as well. The three of them set about pulling and devouring orb after orb, absorbed in a sumptuous feast that it seemed would have no end. Sugarcoat and Sir Sniff arrived just as a mighty burp issued from Nip's throat.

"What in Heaven's name?" Sugarcoat exclaimed. "I thought you were going to wait for us to tell you whether these were safe." All chewing halted as the three diners glanced at each other.

"Uh—," Nip said.

"Yes, yes, we were going to wait," said Tippy, "but they just looked so good, and you know what? They are!! They are incredible, actually. Here," he yanked one off and extended it to Sugarcoat.

"No thank you," said Sugarcoat. "I'd rather not eat poisonous berries. Didn't I say you should stay with them, Sniff? They are too irresponsible to be trusted."

"They're not poison!" Tippy said. "We have eaten at least two dozen apiece and they have done us no harm."

"It takes a sunset and a sunrise and a minimum of ten for the poison to work," she said. "I hope you have not been so unwise too, Billowtail."

"What? We are going to die tomorrow?"

"Now Sugarcoat," Sir Sniff said.

"Well, Sniff, I thought they should know. That way, they will have time to say their good-byes."

"Good-byes? I don't want to say any good-byes," Tippy said, nearly in tears. "I don't want to die! I love life and food and trees and everything, and I am too young to leave it all!"

"Me too," Nip lamented.

"Sugarcoat, there must be some mistake," pleaded Billowtail.

"Now, Sugarcoat," Sir Sniff said. "They've suffered enough. Tell them the truth."

"No, Sniff, they have not suffered nearly enough," the white squirrel countered. "But OK."

"What is it?" asked Billowtail desperately. "What is the truth?"

"The truth is they are called grapes," Sugarcoat said.

"And they are not poisonous?"

"No, they are not poisonous," Sugarcoat said unhappily. "They are used to make a beverage called wine, which has made this place called Burgos famous. I overheard the man who rescued Tippy talking about it. He said he had all the fine wine he could drink in his youth, and now would not be able to afford a single drop, yet he drinks instead from the cup of true joy."

"The man in the brown robe?" Billowtail asked, intently.

"Yes." Sugarcoat pulled a grape from the vine.

"What does that mean?" asked Tippy, licking his fingers, one at a time.

"What?" Sugarcoat asked, turning the grape round and round, as if looking for an ideal spot to sink her teeth in.

"The cup of true joy."

"I don't know exactly." She bit into the skin, and juice flew up into her eye, and she slammed it shut immediately. "Mmmm. Mmmm. You know what? This is an amazing food. Truly, truly amazing."

The five of them set about pulling grapes and stuffing their cheeks with total abandon. No one showed any restraint whatsoever, for there were grapes as far as the eye could see.

Suddenly, a tremendous force whistled past Billowtail's ear and lodged itself in a rootstock, inches from Tippy's tail.

"Whoa!" Tippy exclaimed with wide eyes, pushing his tail down behind him in an effort to reduce its likelihood of being a target.

"Run!" called Sir Sniff, dropping a newly-picked grape, which bounced and rolled into Billowtail's path. Billowtail jumped on top of it and rolled it under his feet for a few seconds before tumbling to the ground. The grape was traveling with such speed it bowled Tippy over, and he too wound up in the mud. Sir Sniff, Sugarcoat and Nip kept running. Another species might have noticed that nearly half of their group was not with them. They might have looked behind to see what had happened to the others. Not squirrels. If you are a squirrel you simply go about saving yourself. Nip, Sugarcoat and Sir Sniff had covered quite a bit of ground, but were far from safe as another arrow went whizzing by, between Nip and Sniff.

"Down! Get down!" Billowtail yelled after them.

But even if the trio heard him from that distance, it was too late. Another arrow found its mark in the stalk of a grapevine after slicing through Sugarcoat's left paw. Now, one might assume that was a good place to be hit, compared to say the shoulder or the gut. But the fact of the matter is, the number of nerve endings in hands and feet make their piercing surprisingly excruciating. The arrow did so much damage before moving to its resting place in some vine thickets, Sugarcoat collapsed in pain and lay writhing on the ground. Another arrow thwacked the ground beside her, splattering mud into her eyes. Sniff and Nip, either oblivious or apathetic, kept running, almost nearing the end of the seemingly endless rows of agriculture. Billowtail thought about getting up to go help Sugarcoat, but he was so petrified, he felt as if his underbelly, knees and palms were mortared to the ground. Plus, for a fleeting moment, he felt that Sugarcoat was not worthy of his help. He remembered that she, just a moment ago, had kept running after he had fallen. Who's to say she would help him, if he had been the one who was shot? But then he remembered all the sound advice she had offered since the journey began, how she was really the first one in his life to care enough about his future to scold him for the ridiculous decisions he might be tempted to make. He owed her something for that. It was either that realization or the indisputable fact that Sugarcoat was highly valuable to the mission that made him peel himself up off the ground and run, as fast as he could, to Sugarcoat's side.

"Here," he panted, lifting her and wrapping his arm around her midsection. "Here, let's hurry and get you out of this open area."

Tippy came up from behind and took her other arm.

"W-w-w-watch my hand!" she told him, limping and leaning on the two of them.

Another arrow sliced the extremely small space between Billowtail's and Sugarcoat's heads. The three squirrels dove into a row of vines, hoping to disappear from sight of the arrows. But the vine keeper had so meticulously done his job pruning, that there was nothing but leafless trunks from the ground to squirrel height. Their only hope was for each of them to hide behind a trunk, one trunk per squirrel since the trunks were so skinny (or maybe the squirrels were fat.) Billowtail got Sugarcoat situated behind hers, while Tippy dashed to the next one, and then Billowtail took his post behind a third.

The three of them hoped to stay put and wait it out, but the arrows just kept coming, and nobody was sure how effective grapevines really were as shields. It was, Billowtail feared, just a matter of time before an arrow split the wood and pierced a squirrel. "We're going to have to get out of here," he hollered.

"I can't," cried Sugarcoat, doubling over in pain. "I won't make it. I'm done for anyway. This wound will not heal."

"Of course it will," said Tippy. "You can't give up."

"I can't run," Sugarcoat said, through her tears. "I don't want to die here, but I can't run."

"We could help you, Sugarcoat," Billowtail shouted, "but we'll be a bigger target if we're together. Can you make it just one vine at a time? I'll just be one vine behind you and Tippy will be one vine ahead. We'll take it at your speed."

"I can't, Billowtail. Go on without me. We can't afford to all take risks. Puttermunch needs you."

"No, Sugarcoat. We're not leaving without you. We can't find Puttermunch without you."

"Here," she said, fumbling with her good paw to unwrap the magic thread from her tail. "You'll need to come get this."

"No, Sugarcoat," Billowtail said. "It's just a wounded paw. You're going to be fine."

"I've lost too much blood, Billowtail. I can't see. Things are getting dark before my eyes."

"No, Sugarcoat!" Tippy yelled.

Billowtail dashed to Sugarcoat. An arrow flew over his head and he immediately regretted taking such a chance. He started to think Sugarcoat might be right. Maybe, for the sake of the mission, Sugarcoat would have to be left behind. But even as he was having these thoughts, he had reached Sugarcoat and lifted her onto his back. She winced in pain as her wounded paw got momentarily trapped between her body and his. Billowtail had never carried anything heavier than a moderate-sized twig before, so he feared he would collapse and suffocate under the weight of someone his own size.

"Ugh, ugh, I can't do this," he grunted. "I can't carry you all the way." He stumbled and fell, with Sugarcoat on top of him. Tippy, who had advanced to the next vine, got down as low as he could and crawled to them.

"Come on," he said, pulling on Billowtail. "You two have got to get up!"

Suddenly, they heard footsteps—slow, heavy footsteps, like that of an archer, coming closer and closer. Tippy lay flat on the ground with his hand over his head, his eyes shut, hoping to camouflage in the red dirt. Billowtail rolled to the nearest vine to hide himself. It was done out of gut instinct, and it made him sick to realize he had left Sugarcoat exposed out there all by herself, whimpering limp on the ground. How could he do such a thing? Just to save himself? What value would his life have from this day forward if he let a friend die?

He had already watched his brothers and sisters die, while he did nothing. Was he going to be the survivor again? But isn't survival what matters most? Even more than friendship? Certainly more than establishing oneself as a hero. Survival. That's all that is necessary. These are the things Billowtail told himself inside his head. And he didn't believe a word of it.

When the footsteps finally stopped, Billowtail was face to face with a set of large toes, strapped onto a thick foot-shaped piece of leather, peeking out from under a brown robe. Billowtail craned his neck slowly and looked up at the towering figure. There was no bow and no arrows. The man stooped and spoke directly to Billowtail.

"Little brother," he said. "I have promised my friend the vine dresser that, if he would put down his bow, I would convince you to allow me to escort you from his property. I further promised him that you would refrain from eating any more of his grapes." He smiled at each one of the squirrels separately, as if each one was the only squirrel in the world. "So, do we have a deal, my little friends?"

The squirrels stared speechless and dumbfounded into the man's eyes. Billowtail could not figure out how he was able to understand the man. It was no mystery for Sugarcoat, since she still had the magic thread wrapped securely around her tail. Billowtail wondered if Tippy understood too. It would appear that he did, since the young round-eyed squirrel began nodding his head wildly at the proposition,

"Oh, my heavens," the man said, gently scooping Sugarcoat up. "It looks like you have quite a painful wound." He cupped her in his hand and walked between the rows of vines until he ran out of vines. Billowtail and Tippy followed close behind. The man sat on a low stone wall, took his rope belt off and untwisted it until he was able to pull out a good sized strand. Then he wrapped it around Sugarcoat's paw. "You're going to be OK," he told her. "You have good friends here to take care of you."

Billowtail was overcome with sorrow upon hearing this. He knew Sugarcoat might very well have been left to die if this man had not come along. Squirrels are miserable, selfish creatures, and Billowtail regretted having been born one. And speaking of selfish creatures, where on earth were Sniff and Nip? Did they have no concern for their fellow squirrels? No. They were squirrels. Loners. Hoarders. Sometimes even worse. There have been squirrels who have eaten their own young. No one that Billowtail knew, but there are stories. Say what you want about the beauty, agility, wit and charming mannerisms of squirrels, but don't try to tell anyone they are selfless, altruistic or philanthropic creatures by nature. Mothers will not raise a "defective" baby. Fathers don't raise their young at all or even seem to care at all what happens to them.

And why should this man, not even of their own species, care for them? Could Great Pinkies have something higher in them, something instinctual or something learned or something given as pure gift?

Billowtail felt tears stinging and pushing at his lower eyelids. Whatever it was this man had, he wanted it. He didn't know if a squirrel could get it, but if it were possible, he would like to possess it.

Sugarcoat's breathing was returning to normal now and she seemed almost peaceful, lying still and quiet in the man's hand. He pulled her into his chest and stooped down, and, with his free hand swept together a pile of leaves and laid Sugarcoat softly on the makeshift bed.

"There now, little friend, you just rest. You're going to be just fine."

Billowtail and Tippy sat down next to Sugarcoat, and then the man sat down too. The squirrels couldn't help staring at the man, who was blocking the setting sun so that all that could be seen of it was a thin glow encircling his head.

Sugarcoat fell asleep with Tippy and Billowtail watching her breathe easier and easier.

"We'll, I best be moving on," the man said "Rest now. Your friend will be OK in the morning."

"She will?" Tippy asked.

The man did not answer in words, but with a smile. It was unclear whether he understood. Likely he was smiling at Tippy's charm. Still, the smile meant "yes" to Tippy. The squirrels watched the man's silhouette grow smaller as he walked down the road, into the giant orange sun.

"What will we do about Sir Sniff and Nip?" Tippy asked.

"We'll find them tomorrow." Billowtail piled leaves on Sugarcoat, covering every part of her but her head to ensure she stayed warm. Then he and Tippy made nests for themselves. Tippy soon fell asleep, but Billowtail kept himself awake, listening to the distant barks of dogs, hoping they would remain distant. His eyelids had grown heavy and sticky by the time the Eastern horizon began to glow, but he had managed to ward off sleep.

CHAPTER NINE

SUSPICIONS

SUGARCOAT WOKE WITH THE SUN, sat up and held her injured paw in her good one. She looked at it, confused, as if she had forgotten what had happened to it and was just learning for the first time. "My hand," she said, unwinding the rope. "It feels like—"

Tippy awoke now and blinked firmly as he watched Sugarcoat unravel the wound dressing. "Maybe you better leave that on," he said.

"Yes," Billowtail agreed. "Give it some time."

"It feels better," Sugarcoat said, continuing the unwrapping. "Much better."

She dropped the dressing to the ground and squeezed and expanded, squeezed and stretched her fingers.

"It's all better," Sugarcoat said. "I thought this wound was going to be the end of me. But a sunrise later, and my paw is nearly back to normal. I don't—I can't—I just don't see how this could be." She made a fist and then released it several times, bringing it closer to her face to inspect her fingers.

"Looks like it will be good as new when the fur grows back," Billowtail said.

"Well, I'd like to find a river," Sugarcoat said. "To rinse off a bit." Her beautiful white fur was matted with dried blood in several places on the right side of her torso and stained pink in others.

"You're not hurt anywhere else, are you?" Billowtail asked.

"No. No," Sugarcoat assured him. "What in the blazes are you doing, Tippy?"

The young squirrel had braided the rope that had bound Sugarcoat's wound and had tied it around his waist. "This is sure to come in handy at some point," he said. "If one of us gets hurt again."

"So, now we have a healing rope, do we?" Sugarcoat smiled. "We have an interpreting thread and a healing rope."

"I don't think it's the rope," Billowtail said. "I think it had something to do with that man." He looked off into the distance, in the direction the man had taken when they last saw him.

"The man?" Tippy asked, tying all kinds of elaborate and unnecessary knots in the tails of the rope that hung from his waist. "But he's not even here."

"He doesn't have to be here," Billowtail said, not understanding exactly what he himself meant by such a statement.

"Speaking of not here," Tippy said, "shouldn't we be looking for Nip and Sir Sniff?"

"Shouldn't they be looking for us?" said Billowtail. It was a statement and not a question.

The three of them set out to find a body of water and a couple of squirrels who had started this journey with them, who could have easily been seen as traitors or, at best, deserters. But there was also a nagging question in the back of all of their minds: what if some ill fate had befallen them?

As it turns out, they found both the squirrels and the body of water at the same time.

"Where have you been?" demanded Sugarcoat.

"We've been finding Puttermunch," said Nip.

"You found him?" asked Billowtail, leaping to his feet.

"Yes!" said Nip.

"Well, where is he?" Tippy asked.

"Let me explain," said Sir Sniff, stepping slightly in front of Nip. "Just as we reached the road, coming out of the field of grapes, the boy came by in his cart. We didn't want to let him get away, so we followed him. When he stopped to bathe in the river, the thirsty cat left the cart, with all her babies inside. We were seconds away from rescuing Puttermunch. We snuck up to the cart and were just about to climb inside when a couple of hound dogs that belong to one of the Great Pinkies came bouncing out of the woods, heading right in our direction, bearing teeth and dripping drool. We ran as fast as we could up a tree and watched from above as the cat shot back into the cart."

"Were you at least able to get a glimpse of Puttermunch?" asked Billowtail.

"Yes," said Sir Sniff. "He looked well-fed and impeccably groomed, a right handsome fellow, who probably gets licked several times a day."

"Well, where is the cart now?" Sugarcoat inquired.

"After the river, the boy took his cart and pressed on, and we followed until he stopped to set up camp. Then, we climbed a tree and watched, hoping the cat would come out again. But she never did, and we fell asleep. When we woke up in the morning, the cart was gone. That's when we decided to come back and try to find the three of you."

"Oh, so you hadn't forgotten about us?" asked Sugarcoat, rather snidely.

"No, of course not," said Sir Sniff. "It's just that it didn't make much sense to come back and get shot at when Puttermunch's cart was passing right before us and we might have had the opportunity to rescue him."

"*Might* have," said Sugarcoat. "Interesting choice of words."

"How so?" asked Sir Sniff, skeptically.

"Sounds hypothetical," Sugarcoat replied, with an equal amount of cynicism.

"What do you mean?"

"Not factual," Sugarcoat stated.

"Are you calling into question our honesty?" Sir Sniff asked grimly.

Sugarcoat stared straight into his eyes. "I am merely saying that it's easy to say such things, but there is no cart or cat or baby squirrel or anything else around to prove it."

"Why should there have to be something offered as proof? I am true to my word. And I resent the implication that we have fabricated events."

"I meant no offense," Sugarcoat said, with a slight bow. "And I am sorry you are insulted. Still, my question was not out of line when directed to someone who left more than half of his alliance behind, in peril."

"I did not think it would do any good for us all to get killed, if that was going to be the fate of one of us."

"Of course it wouldn't," said Sugarcoat coldly.

"Well, all is well now," said Tippy. "We are all together again and none of us is dead."

"Thanks to the man in the brown robe," said Sugarcoat.

"Anyway, Mademoiselle Sugarcoat," Sir Sniff said, in a vaguely sarcastic tone, "all is well that ends well. At least none of us took an arrow through the heart."

"No need!" she exclaimed. "The one through my paw nearly killed me!"

"Your paw? Let me see." He took hold of both her hands and looked at them intently. "Why there's nothing wrong with either one of your paws. What's wrong with you Sugarcoat? I have never known you to be prone to melodrama."

"Melodrama?" Sugarcoat raised the volume on her voice. "Have you any idea what we went through out there? If it wasn't for Billowtail, I would surely be dead."

"Well he might be the first squirrel in the history of squirrelkind to ever save anything but a nut for safekeeping," chuckled Sir Sniff. "We just do not have it in us."

"I must admit, you are right," said Sugarcoat pensively. "So why did you do it, Billowtail?"

"I—I don't know. But I am certainly not a hero, if that's what you're getting at." He didn't want to be branded that way, or else everyone would be expecting him to perform heroic deeds, which was not something he wished to do. "It was that man who saved your life, actually, Sugarcoat. You remember, don't you?"

"Yes, I remember." She looked off to what must have been a dreamy, distant place.

"What man?" asked Nip.

"The one who saved me on the bridge," said Tippy. "He convinced the vine keeper to put down his bow and then bound up Sugarcoat's wound, and it healed almost instantly."

"Hmmm," said Sir Sniff. "Mysterious."

"Do you have a point you wish to make, Sniff? Then make it." Sugarcoat dropped courtesy titles when she was mad, whereas Sir Sniff added them when he got angry.

"An instantly-healed mortal wound. Sounds no more credible than our discovery of Puttermunch's cart. Speaking of which, we are wasting valuable time. Let us be off to find the little tyke."

CHAPTER TEN

DINING WITH MONKS

I JUST HAD A STRANGE THOUGHT," said Billowtail, who was the first in the line of squirrels following the boy's cart.

"What's that?" asked Tippy, following close on Billowtail's heels, hitting the ground with a small stick, in rhythm with his own gait.

"Tippy, if you wouldn't mind terribly, could you leave some space between me and your menacing stick?" Billowtail requested. "I'm afraid you're going to skewer one of my feet."

"Oh, sorry," said Tippy. He dropped back a little—enough to leave room for one squirrel. "Now what was your strange thought?"

"What if Puttermunch doesn't want to be rescued? What if he likes his life here on the road, seeing new places, tasting exotic foods like grapes and barley bread and drinking milk from a domesticated animal?"

"And having his coat licked regularly," Nip added, skipping to catch up with Tippy, smoothing out his own fur with the palms of his hands.

"I am sure that, despite all those luxuries," said Sir Sniff, who followed behind Tippy and Nip. "Puttermunch just wants to go home."

"Me too," said Nip. "There's nothing better than home. And we just keep getting farther and farther away from it."

"Until we reach the midpoint," said Sugarcoat. "Then we shall grow ever nearer."

"How far until the midpoint," asked Tippy.

"That all depends on that incorrigible cat," said Sir Sniff.

It was Sir Sniff they had to thank for the fact that they were following the boy once again. He was able to use his Squirrelish to communicate with a field mouse, who had seen a boy with a cart and horse pass by. Rodents of various species can sometimes understand Squirrelish, much in the same way an Italian can understand a Spaniard. The languages are similar enough, and the field mouse was kind enough to point The Alliance in the right direction at the fork. Running at an exhaustingly swift speed, it wasn't long before the squirrels came upon the cart, and Billowtail, Nip, Sugarcoat, Tippy and Sir Sniff had a new respect for field mice, who have traditionally been looked down upon because of their lowly living conditions.

When the boy stopped along the road to greet a group of resting pilgrims, Sugarcoat was able to learn that they were in a place called Burgos. The boy was supposedly on his way to the San Pedro de Cardeña Monastery to pay his respects to the remains of one of his heroes, El Cid. A fierce debate broke out among the Great Pinkies at the mention of this name. A couple of them had insisted that the knight who became the national hero of Spain was not the admirable figure legend portrayed him to be.

"He was in it for his own gain, plundering and spilling innocent blood—enemy and countrymen alike," one of the men without teeth bellowed. "It made no difference to him. No patriot was he! And no loyal subject of His Holiness!"

"How can you say such things?" another countered. "You have bought what the enemy offers for sale, sullying this brave knight's reputation. For shame!"

"He was a great man – a great father and husband and a moral man, defending Spain against invaders." A third pilgrim chimed in. "Tis a pity we don't have such a man today."

"Aw, we got plenty the likes of him today," said the toothless one. "He was an opportunist. Power hungry, seeking conquest only for his own advancement and wealth. He would fight for whichever side had the most gold to offer."

"I don't care what anybody says," the boy insisted. "My grandfather told me of El Cid's greatness. And he learned it from his grandfather, who knew someone who knew someone who knew brave El Cid personally. I will go pay my respects to the place of his burial. It's only a day's walk off our route, and I will go, even if I must go alone. Plus, it is said that El Cid's horse, Babieca, is also laid to rest there. And that is just too marvelous to pass up." He rubbed his own horse on the nose with one hand, holding the reins with the other. "I would be honored to be buried with Gimblerigg. He is a true and faithful companion."

"I thought El Cid died in Valencia, after the city was besieged," one of the men said, scratching his dirty head. "Thought the poor man starved to death."

"Yes," said the boy, "but then his wife arrived in Burgos on horseback with her husband's body, and he was laid to rest in the Monastery."

"I will go with you, lad," one of the men said

to the boy. "El Cid or no El Cid, I would be happy to pay my respects to those two hundred monks who were killed by invaders two hundred and sixty years ago. Besides, the live monks are known for their kind hospitality, and I could use me some belly timber right about now."

As Sugarcoat remained within earshot of the conversation, making mental notes of everything the Great Pinkies had to say, in case any of it might provide clues necessary now or in the future, the rest of The Alliance attempted to devise a plan to get into the cart without being noticed. Before the squirrels could think up any rescue plans, the cart was on the move again.

The monks' reputation at the monastery of San Pedro de Cardeña proved to be accurate, and all the travelers were well-fed. A couple of the brothers even threw out some stale crusts and fish heads for Billowtail and the others after marveling at how inspiring it was to see such a variety of pelts on a group of tree squirrels. Billowtail decided to stick with the bread. He had never eaten anything with eyes. Not even an insect. Though squirrels are typically omnivores, Billowtail considered himself a vegetarian. He always felt bad about eating someone's kin, especially if it had a mother waiting for it to come home. He had watched his fellow squirrels' occasional raid on a bird's nest, making a meal of eggs or hatchlings. A mother bird's despair is very much like poor Mrs. Poggins' agony when Puttermunch fell from the nest.

Nip and Tippy managed to pack in the most food, probably twice as much as anyone else.

"What a feast!" Tippy observed, holding the silvery fish head in his hand and taking large bites out of it. "You've got to try this, Billowtail. You're not going to get anything like this back home."

"It is exquisite," Nip agreed, biting into his third fish head. "Would be worth the trip if we never did find Puttermunch."

"Nip!" Sugarcoat scolded, licking her fingers one by one, as she sat beside a pile of picked-clean fish bones. "What a callous thing to say."

"Oh, you know I didn't mean it that way," Nip said. "I want to find the little guy as much as anyone."

Sugarcoat seemed to take little comfort in this, though Billowtail concluded Nip must be sincere. Why else would he have come on this journey? Surely he could not have predicted the fish heads. It seemed to Billowtail that Sugarcoat was suspicious of Sir Sniff and Nip—or at least suspicious of their motives—ever since the vineyard.

"Well, just to clear up any misunderstanding," Sugarcoat stated. "I would like to extend an invitation to anyone who is not wholeheartedly interested in the mission we have before us. Namely, finding Puttermunch and returning him to his mother. I wish you safe travels on your return trip home."

CHAPTER ELEVEN

A GLIMPSE OF PUTTERMUNCH

N O ONE WAS SURE HOW, but the boy slipped away again. Most likely, while the squirrels were feasting on fish heads, enjoying a bit of dinner entertainment. Tippy had pushed fish eyeballs onto a Y-shaped stick and was delivering a soliloquy in a fish voice, telling a tale of woe about how a seemingly innocuous and delicious breakfast worm turned out to be the death of him.

And so the squirrels walked, in the pouring rain, with nothing to follow. There is one thing squirrels share with cats – their disdain for getting wet. Billowtail's teeth had reached chatter point, his fur dripping in drenched misery. At this point, he wasn't even sure The Alliance was heading in the right direction. Last Sugarcoat heard, the boy was taking a detour to yet another monastery in a town called Santo Toribio de Liébana. The theory was that he was going there to see some kind of relic.

"What is a relic?" Nip asked.

"I don't know," said Sugarcoat. "But I heard the boy tell one of his traveling companions that night in Burgos that he was going to see the largest one of its kind."

It was really a journey of faith at this point. The only way the squirrels had of knowing they were on the road to their destination was by picking up bits and pieces of conversation, such as the one overheard several days ago when one of the pilgrims asked another, "How much farther to Santo Toribio?"

Beyond even the question of going in the right direction, there was the question of whether Puttermunch was even still with the boy.

"It would be easier to trudge all this way if we could just know there was a baby squirrel somewhere in front of us," complained Nip.

"Shhh, wait a minute," said Sugarcoat stopping and holding her arms out, so no one could pass. "Listen!"

The squirrels stood like statues and cocked their heads, as if waiting for sound to pour from the sky into their ears. (Fortunately, they had travelled out from under the rain or they would have surely contracted a bad case of swimmer's ear.)

"Meow," came a faint statement from the north.

"Is that our cat?" whispered Tippy excitedly.

"Shhh," insisted Sugarcoat. "Listen!"

"That's her," Sir Sniff confirmed in a whisper.

Human laughter lilted past the goose-high grass on the side of the road. The squirrels soft-pawed along that edge of the road until there came a break in the grass and they could see, as difficult as it was for them to believe their eyes, a teen boy, playing with a litter of kittens in a small clearing surrounded by elderly trees. The boy was sitting on the rock, with mewing kittens climbing all over him. He picked up first one and then the other, stroking the full length of its back.

The squirrels held their spots behind the grass, not daring to venture into view of feline or human. They all knew cats were bad news because Lady Flora had educated them on the dangers of whiskered sorts, but nobody knew exactly what a kitten would do with a squirrel. What kind of standoff would it be? Would it involve tooth or nail or a combination of the two? And who would reign victorious?

"Does he have food?" Nip asked, peeking through a thick row of tall grass. "Why are those kittens so fond of him?

"Where's Puttermunch?" Billowtail asked.

"Shhh." answered Sugarcoat. "Maybe still in the cart or something."

"Or up in a tree," whispered Nip, scanning the leaves that made a canopy around the perimeter of the meadow.

"Not likely," Sir Sniff said. "He's still just a little one."

Billowtail had lost track of the passage of time. Squirrels were normally pretty good at knowing time. But then again, they normally stay in one place. There was something about adding movement to the equation. When both time and space are in motion, it seems to throw off a squirrel's inner clock. Sir Sniff came to understand this early in the journey and took up the practice of tying a knot in one of his whiskers each time the sun set. It had required twenty-seven knots to come this far.

"There he is!" cried Tippy. "There's Puttermunch!"

The squirrels all looked at Tippy to see where he was looking, and then looked at what he was looking at. Their eyes were rewarded with a vision of the most beautiful young squirrel they had ever seen. Possibly even the most beautiful vision they had ever seen anywhere of anything. The cat lay on her side, soaking in the sun that had broken through the clouds, lifting her head to watch her own tail twitch gracefully this way and that. Even more interested in her tail than the cat herself was wee Puttermunch, who scampered around it and bat at it each time it moved.

"Thank Heavens!" said Billowtail, picturing an overjoyed Mrs. Poggins gathering the tiny squirrel into her arms, shedding tears of relief at his home-coming.

"I can't believe the little muncher is alive!" said Tippy.

"Miracle of miracles!" exclaimed Sir Sniff.

"Look how much hair he has!" said Nip.

"He's fully furred," said Sugarcoat, proudly, as if she had something to do with the filling in of his coat.

"Handsome fellow!" said Sir Sniff, very pleased indeed.

"Well, what are we waiting for!" said Tippy. "Let's go get him!"

"Wai—wai—wai—wai—wait!" said Sir Sniff, grabbing Tippy's tail to keep him from charging. "You can't just go rushing up to a cat and expect her not to make breakfast out of you."

"It's too late in the day for breakfast," Tippy pointed out, somewhat annoyed that his plans were foiled by an overly-cautious elder.

"Supper then," said Sir Sniff, with a subtle nod of the head to admit his error.

"Well, she hasn't eaten Puttermunch," Billow-tail said.

"Yes, but you know what the Great Pinkies said," Sugarcoat reminded him. "It's an odd thing that she doesn't. She must see him as one of her own."

"Or she's fattening him up so she can make a good meal out of him," said Sir Sniff.

Puttermunch scampered to the front of the cat now and playfully jumped at her shoulders, trying to start a rumble. The cat snuzzled her nose into Puttermunch's haunch and licked half the length of him, pasting patches of his new fur flat onto his plump bulb of a body.

"See!" said Sir Sniff. "She's tasting him!"

"So, what's our plan, squirrels?" said Nip. "We're wasting valuable time."

"One of us should approach and see if she's friendly or hostile," said Tippy.

"And who might volunteer for that?" asked Sir Sniff.

Nip and Sugarcoat looked at each other with sideways glances, cast in between examinations of their own feet and the tiny mounds of mud they were displacing with their clenched toes.

"Me," said Tippy. "I'm not afraid of her."

"What?" No," said Sugarcoat. "That's no good. We are not going to sacrifice any one of us."

"Let's all go together then," said Sir Sniff.

"I don't like that idea," said Sugarcoat. "If we all get eaten, there'll be no one to rescue Puttermunch."

"Sort of like if we all got shot by arrows?" Sir Sniff said.

"Touché, Sir Sniff," said Sugarcoat, "but now is not the time to re-hash bygone decisions."

"Well, she can't eat all of us at once," said Tippy.

"But she can eat some of us and slice the remainder of us with her razor sharp claws," said Sir Sniff.

Squirrels are not aware of the power they have in numbers as they are not inclined to team projects.

"You are forgetting she is not a wild animal." Tippy said. "You see how pleased she is to let the

Great Pinky touch her kittens. How vicious can she be?"

"She has taken quite good care of Puttermunch," said Nip. "She must be a creature of good will."

"Look, none of us is an expert on pets," Sugarcoat said. "We have had no contact with them. So we just don't know what we're in for. We have to exercise the utmost caution. We can't afford to lose any one of us. And yet we can't afford to lose all of us either."

Suddenly, as if talking about "one" and "all" triggered a reminder in them that they were supposed to be five squirrels, they all noticed at the same time that they were only four. Billowtail had left the debate in favor of taking action. And that action was about to unfold right in the shadow of a tabby cat's whiskers.

CHAPTER TWELVE

THE UNBEARABLE LOSS

GOOD EVENTIDE!" Billowtail said, standing in his best posture, smiling nervously up into the cat's face. "I come as friend, not foe, and I wish to have a word with you. We thank you for your kind service to our beloved Puttermunch, and we have come now to return him to his grieving mother."

The remainder of The Alliance froze in shock.

"What is he talking at that cat for, as if she speaks Squirrelish," said Sir Sniff.

"Look!" said Nip. "He's got the magic thread!"

"Why, that little—" but before Sugarcoat could get the insult out of her mouth, the cat lunged and planted her forepaw right into Billowtail's torso, pinning him to the ground. Billowtail screeched and squirmed beneath the oppressive weight, his eyes bulging with a mixture of fear and oxygen deprivation.

Puttermunch took off running, disappearing

into the trees.

A collective gasp went up amongst Billowtail's comrades, and then a sudden, desperate inspiration washed over them, so foreign to squirrel ideology, no one knew where the idea had come from, but there wasn't time for questioning. Maybe if they had grown up in a pride as lions or in a pack as wolves or a flock as birds, the idea might not have been so absurd. But even as they were rushing toward the ferocious cat, they were thinking themselves to be certifiably insane. They were risking their lives for a friend.

Mud flew as the squirrels charged at the cat, scuffling a cloud of confusion into her menacing face. Billowtail sputtered as his captor removed her paw from his midsection and sliced at the air, striking at the flurry of danger that had overtaken her and releasing Billowtail, who struggled to get to his feet. The cat made another attempt, swatting into the jumble of squirrels. Her claw came within hair's width of Sir Sniff's ear. Billowtail started to scurry away from the fray, bound in the direction Puttermunch had fled, making the calculation that it was best to make the rescue while the cat had her mind on other things, lest they never find the little one again. Noticing that her original catch was getting away, the determined feline swiped at Billowtail, missing his haunch, but snagging the magic thread with one of her toenails. He struggled to get free, yanking his ankle from the thread's grip, leaving it hooked on the cat's claw.

"Retreat!" cried Sir Sniff. "Into the woods!"

The cat lodged her final hissing complaint, mouth wide open and lips raised above her hideous fangs, as all five squirrels bolted for the trees, once again pursued by arrows. The boy, no doubt, saw an opportunity to rid the world of these strange and vicious pet-attacking squirrels and at the same time procure some meat for his next meal.

The squirrels ran so far into the trees, they came out the other side into a village they assumed must be Liébana.

They stopped at the edge of the village, panting and doubling over with exhaustion.

They had come so close to nabbing Puttermunch, but now they had no idea where he had gone. The worst of it was that the cat now had the magic thread and there was no telling what damage a cat could do if she were to understand what humans have to say. Lady Flora had told them that it is widely believed that cats aspire to world domination, if they only had the tools.

Sugarcoat remembered what she was told when she was given the magic thread, and the words sliced into her with every bit as much pain as the cat might have inflicted.

Keep this great gift from the claws of evil.

Sugarcoat had clearly failed.

She was angry with Billowtail for his irresponsibility. But she was even angrier with herself for not keeping the thread better guarded. But there were no wells or ponds or lakes or puddles immediately available to look into and scold her own reflection. So Billowtail would receive the brunt of her wrath.

"Billowtail, you have failed us miserably. How could you? You know you are never to touch the magic thread. No one is to lay a paw on the magic thread! You have been impulsive and foolish."

"I know, Sugarcoat. I am sorry. I only wanted to help."

"You wanted to help yourself to glory. You were trying to be a hero. Look where that got us. Now we have no way of knowing what the humans are saying, the thread lies in enemy paws, and we have again lost Puttermunch with no way to find him."

"I'm sorry. I wish I could go back and do it all different."

"Ridiculous wishes fix nothing, Billowtail," Sugarcoat snarled. "I think you should go home."

"Home?" Billowtail took his eyes off his own feet now and looked first to Sugarcoat and then to Sir Sniff.

"We're not playing a game here, Billowtail," said Sir Sniff calmly. "We are trying to save a life. We can't afford to make mistakes born of ego and pride."

"We can't send him home," said Tippy. "He meant well."

"He was brave," Nip said. "He faced the cat none of the rest of us wanted to."

"Yeah, with no planning whatsoever," Sugarcoat said. "Look at the mess he got us into."

"I'm feeling a little strange," Tippy said. "Do you think we could find some water?"

"Tippy!" cried Nip. "You are bleeding!"

Now everyone looked at Tippy for the first time since the retreat into the woods. Tippy looked down over his torso, which was gashed in dual parallel lines from left shoulder to right hip, in the shape of a royal sash. "Just a little cat bite," he said with a weak smile. "It will heal."

"Tippy!" exclaimed Billowtail, scurrying over to his friend, taking him by the arm and guiding him to a soft bed of leaves. "Here sit down."

"Hey," said Sugarcoat. "Where is the rope, Tippy? The one that Brown Robe wrapped around my paw?"

"Oh," said Tippy. "I think I left it a few miles back."

"More than a few, I'll bet," said Sugarcoat. "I told you and Nip you shouldn't be playing with it."

"I'm sorry," said Tippy. "But please, can someone get me water?"

"I will go find you some," Billowtail assured him.

"Not so fast, Billowtail," Sugarcoat barked.

"Have you learned nothing? Consult, Billowtail! Consult with your group."

"No need to consult," came an unfamiliar voice. "Somebody should get the poor boy some water. You've got to just strive to keep him comfortable at this point."

They all looked at the stranger with bewildered stares.

"Izzy Twiggens," said a tailless black squirrel, stepping fully from behind a tree trunk, placing his hand on his chest. "Thought I'd see if I could be of service. Saw the whole thing from my tree. Sorry about your friend. Tippy, is it?"

Now a squirrel without a tail is quite a rarity, and under normal circumstances, thoughts of what might have happened to the missing tail would occupy the mind. But Alliance minds were already fully occupied.

Izzy Twiggens took a few timid steps closer, and placed his paw on Tippy's arm. "You put up a valiant fight there. That makes you a winner in the end. Even if it is the end."

"Thank you, Sir," Tippy said weakly. "I'm just really thirsty now. If someone could get me some water, I'm sure I'd feel good as new."

"Sure, friend, sure. Brave lad you are. C'mon Billowtail, I know where there's a fountain."

Billowtail looked at Sugarcoat and then Sir Sniff.

"Go on, son," Sir Sniff nodded.

"Right away. I'll be quick." He took about a dozen steps and stopped in his tracks. "Oh, uh, what should I carry the water in?"

"You should be able to find an acorn somewhere," said Sugarcoat. "Use the shell."

"I'll help you, lad," Izzy Twiggens said. "If you can't find one straight away, my drey is close by, and I've got a stocked pantry."

Billowtail's stomach would have normally been

rumbling at the mention of a pantry, especially a full one, but he felt nothing but a nauseating remorse in the pit of his gut.

"Sorry about your friend," the black squirrel said as he led Billowtail along the perimeter of the village green, flanked by a number of thatch-roofed huts and various sizes and shapes of Great Pinkies going about a variety of business and leisure pursuits—hitching oxen to plows, knocking over pins with a ball, loading up wagons with parsnips. "Seems like such a nice fella."

"Tippy? Yes, he is one of the bravest squirrels I know. What he did for me could have cost him his life."

Izzy Twiggens stopped abruptly and turned to face Billowtail. "You don't know, do you?"

"Know what?"

"Wait a minute. Wait a minute. Where are you from?"

"From Bon Arbre, far away, over the mountains, across many roads and over more mountains."

"You don't have cats where you come from, do you?"

"No, we rarely even see a Great Pinky, much less any of their pets. We've seen an occasional hunting dog, though. My uncle was even bitten by one. Lost his front left paw. My mother had to bring him nuts and eggs from then on. He never was able to harvest very well for himself. I'm sure glad Tippy has all his limbs intact."

"Well, I don't know how to break this to you, young lad. But cats aren't dogs. Squirrels lose much more than their limbs when they are bit by a cat."

"What do you mean?"

"Cat bites are fatal."

"Fatal?! What does fatal mean?"

"I'm sorry, Billowtail. Your friend's not going to

see the next sunset."

"What do you mean? He's going to die? But it's just a little bite."

"There is something in a cat's saliva that is deadly to squirrels. We here in these parts are taught that from pinky up. But I guess you back-woods squirrels have no reason for knowing it. I'm sorry to be the one to have to tell you. And under these circumstances too. Such a pity."

"No, you've got to be mistaken. Something has got to be done. Tippy has to live." The normally soft-spoken Billowtail heard his own voice take on an uncommon intensity. It was as if he thought if he spoke loudly enough somebody might be able to change something.

"There's nothing that can be done, Billowtail. No squirrel has ever been known to survive a cat bite."

Billowtail burst into tears now. "If he dies, it will be all my fault. He can't die. It should be me, not him. Why couldn't it have been me?"

"Oh, my friend, life deals us some difficult things to bear sometimes." Izzy lay a hand on Bil-lowtail's shoulder and tried to look into his face, which Billowtail had covered with his hands. "But you have to accept it and go on, the best way you know how."

"I don't know how!" Billowtail wailed. "This isn't difficult. It's impossible. I can't bear this. I just can't."

"You can bear it, son. And you will. It's a dev-astating loss to say the least, but you've got the strength in you. I see it. I see it clear."

CHAPTER THIRTEEN

ON EAGLE'S WING

IZZY TWIGGENS SCOOPED water from the fountain into the acorn cap and passed it to Billowtail. "Here, this will make Tippy more comfortable. Let's hurry and get it back to him."

"I can't go back." Billowtail returned the water to Izzy. "You'll have to take it to him. I can't go back there."

"You have to go back, lad. Your friends are depending on you."

"They are much better without me. Tippy doesn't even know yet he's going to die. And Sugarcoat and Nip and Sniff, I'm sure they will hate me when they find out."

"But you can't abandon your friends when they need you. Like I said, life gives us tough things to bear. Friends make it bearable."

"I am no friend to them. I am pure suffering. I have cost them dearly. I have cost Tippy everything."

"And would you have not done the same for him? Would you not lay down your life for him, just as he did for you?"

"Yes. Of course I would."

"Then you understand. Tippy has paid the cost of love. And he will have no regrets."

Izzy took Billowtail by the arm and gently led him along the pathway back toward the trees where The Alliance waited.

"If only we still had the healing rope," Billowtail muttered.

"Hmmm?"

"It was a rope that this man in a brown robe wrapped around Sugarcoat's paw. Her wound was gone by sunrise."

"I'm afraid Tippy doesn't have one of those kinds of wounds, Billowtail. I know it's difficult for you to accept it, but there is nothing that can help your friend."

The face of the man in the brown robe lingered in Billowtail's mind, and he wished there was some way to find him. It might have been possible to believe that no *thing* could save Tippy. But it would be difficult to believe that no *one* could.

As they neared the encampment, there was a strange quiet, as if everyone was sleeping or in deep sadness, and Billowtail got the horrible feeling that Tippy had passed.

But there in the small clearing, with all the squirrels gathered around, was the most beautiful sight.

"He came!" Billowtail wanted to holler, but his throat was tight with disbelief, so it just came out as a whisper. "He really came!"

Billowtail and Izzy froze in their tracks and dropped their jaws, standing perfectly still in silent awe of the man in the brown robe cradling Tippy in his hand. Nothing could have been more beautiful.

Nothing could have inspired more happiness, deep within Billowtail's heart, a place where there had been such pain.

And then the brown-robed man, lifting Tippy up to the level of his own eyes and holding him out away from his kind face, let out a whistle that sounded something like the call of a lark.

Billowtail thought maybe the man, unaware that squirrels do not speak Birdish, was trying to communicate with Tippy. Within seconds, an eagle swooped in, as if from nowhere, and using its massive talons, snatched Tippy right from the man's hand. Tippy seemed to go limp, from what they could tell from the ground, as the hideous creature lifted effortlessly into the sky.

"Nooooo! Tippy!" Billowtail yelled, craning his neck and running after the eagle until it reached the end of the clearing, sailed over the trees and disappeared from sight. Then Billowtail could think of nothing to do but run around and around the perimeter of the clearing until he dropped from pure exhaustion. Actually it was from lack of oxygen as his heart beat faster than his lungs could breathe. All the squirrels rushed to Billowtail's side. Sir Sniff grabbed one arm and Nip grabbed the other, and they helped him to his feet, though he didn't consider it very helpful because he wanted to lie there forever.

Sugarcoat made a slow, 360-degree survey of the meadow. "He's gone," she reported. "The man in the brown robe is gone."

"What are we going to do?" cried Nip.

"There's nothing we can do, son," said Sir Sniff, hanging his head.

"We have to go after that eagle!" Nip insisted.

"Eagles travel so much faster than we squirrels could ever hope to," said Sugarcoat. "In fact, they're probably nearly to world's end by now."

"Well, the eagle could be," said Izzy Twiggens.

"I doubt he will carry Tippy too long without consuming him."

A gasp went up.

"Well, surely you squirrels of Bon Arbre have heard of birds of prey."

"Of course," Sugarcoat said. "We just—it's just—"

"It's difficult thinking about one of your friends being eaten, I know," Izzy said.

"We've all grown quite close on this journey," said Sir Sniff, dabbing at his eyes.

Billowtail could not begin to fathom how someone so gentle and kind as the brown-robed man would do such a thing to a poor defenseless animal.

"I am very sorry for your loss," said Izzy Twiggens. "But maybe it is better this way. Your friend won't have to suffer as long."

"What?" Sugarcoat demanded. "What are you talking about? It was only a scratch."

"Cat bites are fatal," Izzy Twiggens informed. "Tippy was going to be dead within twenty-four hours anyway."

Billowtail wished in the depth of his gut that Izzy could have kept that detail to himself. A few minutes ago, he would have been grateful that someone else is breaking the horrible news about fatal cat bites. But now the information seemed irrelevant and unnecessary. And yet, even with the two fatal events that poor Tippy had been dealt, Billowtail could not let go. Tippy had last been seen alive, not dead.

"We have to go after him," Billowtail sobbed. "We have to try to find him."

"I don't see how we could, Billowtail," Sir Sniff said. "Eagles can fly sixty miles an hour. We squirrels can only cover twenty on a good day, with the wind at our backs."

"So, we're just going to give up on him?" Billowtail could hardly get the words out. He was fully aware his voice came out as a desperate squeak.

"You are in no place to become sanctimonious over this, Billowtail," Sugarcoat said sternly. "It is because of you that Tippy is lost to us. That eagle took him because he was injured. And that's because of you. And now Mr. Twiggens here tells us he was good as dead already because of the cat bite. And that he owes to you as well."

"Sugarcoat! That will be enough," Sir Sniff declared. "Can't you see Billowtail already feels bad enough. Leave the poor kid alone."

"No, let her talk," Billowtail pushed the words out through his tears. "She is right."

"I'm sorry, Billowtail," Sugarcoat said. "It's just that I had grown quite fond of Tippy. As all of you had, I am sure."

"What about the brown-robed man?" Nip asked. "Would he help us? I mean, if we can find him." He looked around the clearing.

"Help us?" Sugarcoat barked. "Where have you been, Nip? That so-called kind man just fed our friend to an eagle."

"No," said Billowtail. "Do not dismiss Nip's suggestion so quickly. Please. Maybe the brown-robed man could be convinced. Maybe if he knew how much we—" The remainder of the sentence filled his throat and could not push its way past the tears. "He's the one who saved me from the dog." He took a gulp as his tears trickled back into his throat. "And Sugarcoat from the mortal arrow wound. And Tippy from the bridge."

"Then, why would he do such an evil thing to poor Tippy now?" asked Sugarcoat

"Maybe he was trying to put him out of his misery," said Sir Sniff.

"Maybe he loved his hawk friend more," offered Sugarcoat

"It was an eagle," Sir Sniff corrected her.

"Yes, excuse me. An eagle."

"How are we going to tell Tippy's poor mother?" Billowtail lamented. "We don't even have a body for a proper burial."

"We shall hold a memorial even still," Sir Sniff said. "When we return to Bon Arbre, we shall."

"Oh, why couldn't it have been me?" said Billowtail. "I don't have a mother to tell. Wouldn't it have made more sense if it were me?" Billowtail put his hands over his eyes and resumed his crying.

"There, there, Billowtail, you've got to get hold of yourself," said Sir Sniff, placing a paw on his shoulder. "Remember, we still have little Puttermunch to think about. We don't want our friend to have died in vain."

Billowtail shook his head. "I am of no use to anybody here. I will only put you in harm's way. I'm going home. I will break the news to Mrs. Whimtucket and offer myself as her slave for the rest of my life. It is no consolation for the loss of a son, but it is the only thing I can offer."

"That is very brave, Billowtail," said Sugarcoat. "I must say. Very brave"

"Brave? I thought you'd think me a coward for turning back."

"I think your wanting to take care of Mrs. Whimtucket is the most valiant I've seen you. The problem is, we are down to four and if you leave we'll be only three. I don't know if we can rescue Puttermunch without you."

"I concur," said Sir Sniff. "I think you best press on, Billowtail. We need you."

"Need me? I've been nothing but trouble the whole trip. More than trouble. I've brought everyone tragedy. Maybe Izzy Twiggens can take my place."

"Take your place? No, no one can take another's place, lad," the tailless squirrel said. "I would be happy to oblige and join your Alliance, but I am just too old for such a mission. I wouldn't make it a single league. In my youth, I would have jumped at the chance. I saw many an exciting moments in my day, I did. Danger and adventure! In my head, that is. I always dreamed of such things, but never have I been given the opportunity. Not 'til this moment anyway. And now I am too old and rickety. What rotten luck."

"I wish I were old and rickety," said Nip. "Sounds safer than being young and able."

"I am no kit myself," said Sir Sniff. "But with age, comes invaluable wisdom. You can come along as an advisor. We would be honored to have you."

"I'm afraid I wouldn't be able to keep up. Without a tail to keep my balance, I'd go down like a stone."

None of the squirrels could imagine going through life tailless. They relied on their tails for so many things, including definition of personality. Yet, Izzy Twiggens did not seem to lack any of that. He seemed so spry and lively, it was almost as if one could see his tail, even though it did not exist.

"How'd you lose it?" Nip asked.

"Nip!" scolded Sugarcoat. "That's not polite."

"That's OK," said Izzy Twiggens, giving Nip's hair a tussle. "Curiosity is the sign of an active mind, right Nip? You want to hear the tale of the tail, do ya? Well, to make a very long story short, I got in a scuffle with a dog when I was about your age. I escaped with my life, and all that hound got was a mouth full of tail."

"So you've lived all this time without it." Nip said.

"Really had no other choice," said Izzy, "although for a number of years, I was waiting for it to grow back, even though I'd never known of such a thing to really happen. Finally, I came to accept I was never going to get a new tail. And that's when my life began."

"But aren't you cold in winter?"

"I might be, if it wasn't for the goodwill of my neighbors, who have contributed extra leaves and twigs and even hair from their own tails to line my nest. Yeah, indeed, they've been taking care of me ever since my beloved Rosebud died."

"You had a rosebud, uh, I mean a wife?" Nip asked.

"I met her in the fall, many falls ago. Her tail provided shelter for the both of us for seven seasons and we raised twenty-four little ones together all in total. I am a fortunate squirrel to have had her for so long."

"Wow," said Nip. "She let you stay with her?"

"Year after year."

"In the same nest with her and the babies?"

"She would never have turned me out into the cold. Keep in mind, my Rosebud was no ordinary doe. You know how most lady squirrels are. Always looking for the buck with the fanciest tail antics. That's how you impress them. Everybody knows that. So, I didn't stand a chance at winning anyone's affection. Or so I thought. But Rosebud saw past what I didn't have and looked right into the heart of what I did have. A doe like that is all heart. She even let me help look after our kits. I watched them all grow up. I dare say, if I had a tail, I never would have been so fortunate."

Billowtail was hearing all this, but not listening. No thought and no idea that had anything to do with something other than Tippy's loss was going to penetrate the grief that had enveloped him. He lay face-first on the ground, paws outstretched, palms to the dirt. He wanted to dissolve into dust. He could not imagine rising up again. Something inside him told him he must. But he was not going to listen. He hadn't the strength to listen. Any strength he had would be used to will himself to seep into oblivion. To trickle down into nothing-ness. Deep, deep into what never has been.

"C'mon, Chico, up on your feet."

Billowtail lifted his eyebrows and then his eyes and then his head, just slightly, just enough to see the face that had dared to believe he was capable of rising.

"C'mon." Izzy Twiggens reached out his paw to Billowtail. "C'mon, just one step at a time, lad. Just one step at a time."

CHAPTER FOURTEEN

REMEMBERING MOMMA

BILLOWTAIL HAD FOUND a nice dark corner and intended to stay there until he was sure Sugarcoat, Sir Sniff and Nip had gone on without him. It won't take long, he reasoned, for them to decide they shouldn't waste time looking for him when Puttermunch might be getting farther and farther away. Before the cat snatched the thread, Sugarcoat had heard the boy talk about a place called Compostela. That's where The Alliance will head if they lose the cat's trail. But not Billowtail. He had decided he would be too much of a liability to the group. He lacked desire to go on. And he lacked the courage to go back. There would be too much bad news to bear and too many questions to answer. So he stayed still. He resolved to live in his new little corner until his last day. There seemed to be something safe about the place. Sad, but safe. He had found it while everyone else was napping in nearby trees, exhausted from the grief of losing Tippy. He snuck into the stone building when the arched door opened for a lame man to be carried through. It was difficult to see, as it reminded him of poor Tippy.

Billowtail's corner was in an alcove ablaze with candles. He watched people, one by one, proceed down the center aisle between all the long benches that stretched right and left from the middle. The visitors approached a man in a tall hat, seated in a velvet chair, holding a piece of wood. They got to their knees and placed their lips on the wood for a moment, then placed their hand to their forehead, to their chest and to each shoulder. He knew enough about Great Pinkies, after these many miles on the journey with them, to know that they pressed their lips to other Great Pinkies for whom they seem to feel affection. Why they would be doing this to a piece of wood was mystifying, but they all seemed to love the wood, like they love the person they kiss. Billowtail himself was very fond of wood, as it is the stuff that trees are made of and trees provide shelter and bear nuts. But he couldn't say he *loved* wood. He certainly would never think to kiss it. Gnaw it, yes. But not kiss it.

In late afternoon, there was a lull in visitors to the wood and then a sole man approached. He went down on his knees for a long time, much longer than the others, and after kissing the wood, whispered something lengthy and deep. Billowtail felt it, though he could not comprehend it. He felt it like one feels the wind, and he understood as much about it as he understood the wind. He felt himself drawn to the wood and wished he could approach it alongside the gray-robed man, but he dare not be so bold. He watched as the man left. Then he found himself dissolving again in tears.

The shadows grew long across the dusty floor, scuffed with the prints of Great Pinkies' shoes. Silent hours passed—silent save for the sound of his own sniffling, which he stifled under his tail, so no one could hear it in the almost perfect silence. He curled into a ball, under his tail, using it more for disappearing than for warmth. He wished to vanish from the face of the earth. He fell asleep and dreamed of home, of simpler times, though they never seemed so back then. When he awoke, all the people were gone and the man in the pointy hat placed the beloved wood in a shiny box. Two men in gray robes bowed and one of them took the box and placed it on a tall table flanked with candles. He inserted a long gold key into a hole in the front of the box and wiggled, trying to turn it first one direction, then another. Then he passed it to the other man, who did the same. They both shook their heads and then one of them pointed to an inside door, which the other one went through. The one who remained reopened the box, kissed the wood, closed the box and knelt before it. Billowtail came out of his corner and stood for a long moment, watching the man, whose eyes were closed and lips moving, but Billowtail could not hear anything coming out of the man's mouth. It seemed unreasonable to think he was talking to the wood. Then again, if he loved it enough to kiss it, maybe he was. Billowtail recalled his neighbor, the late Whim Drucker, who used to start every day by popping his head out of his drey, saying "good morning fine tree, may you live until the world's last day for your generosity in sheltering me, giving me warmth and granting me sleep." How Billowtail wished he had never left Bon Arbre. He blamed Sir Sniff for allowing him to go, for assuming he could rise to the occasion. What an unwise elder he was. He should have noticed Billowtail's immaturity and imprudence. Billowtail still did not know why he volunteered to go. It was a good question Lady Flora had asked and still he did not know the answer. What was he hoping to find? Puttermunch, of course. But what else?

Suddenly, a pain stabbed at him, not a pain of the flesh, but one of the heart, and he wanted to cry again. This time, it wasn't because of Tippy, but because of Puttermunch. He felt the aloneness, the aching longing, that the little squirrel must be feeling for his Momma. Billowtail ached, too, for his. Even still, this many seasons later. All he wanted, the whole time he was growing up, was her. His aunt had raised him, but not happily. She provided food, but no affection. She gave him shelter, but no love. His mother had given her life for him, the ultimate sign of love, but then he would have her love no more. He got all of her love in one dose. After that, there was nothing left to give.

The gray-robed man who had disappeared through a door, now returned and shook his head at the one who had been kneeling at the shiny box. The one whispered something in the other's ear and pointed to the rows of pews. Then they both found a spot in the back, near the door. One knelt and one sat. And there they stayed until dark. The only light came from the two candles on each side of the shiny box.

Billowtail ventured slowly down the aisle toward them, keeping to the shadows of the pews. He wanted to test how observant the men were. Their eyes were still closed, and he thought one or maybe both of them might be asleep.

He decided to take his chances. He stole back up the aisle and scampered up the leg of the table and behind the box. Standing on his two back feet, he pressed his hands to one of the hinges that held the lid of the box in place. He tried to peek in, but it was shut tight. He wondered if he could lift the lid. He normally would have discounted such a notion, but he had found himself, on this journey, to be much stronger physically than he ever thought he was. He noticed that the key the gray robes had tried was still lying on the table. So he grabbed it and wedged it, little by little, wiggling it in between the box and the lid, right where the key clasp was. This opened the box enough for him to slip his arm in, up to his shoulder, and he was able to rest his hand on the wood.

Billowtail fancied himself an expert on trees, as most squirrels are. He had seen many types of wood, both back home in the forest and along the journey to find Puttermunch. He could have closed his eyes and sniffed and told you what kind of tree he was sniffing. He could have identified any tree with his eyes closed, just by running his hand over its bark. He could have conducted a quick examination of a cross section of a branch and told you how old it was and how much rain fell during the various years of its life. He could even close his eyes and listen to the wind blowing through the leaves and tell you what kind of tree the leaves belong to. But he had never known any wood like what lay inside the box. It wasn't very big. Maybe about the length of two small squirrels laid tail to nose. But it seemed, to him, to come from a far-away, powerful place. It seemed to pack something very large into something very small. It seemed something was missing, yet it contained everything. Of course, Billowtail had no words for all of this. He just had wordless feelings. He ran his fingers across it and found a hole. He wanted to cry out in longing for his mother. He didn't cry out on the day of her death because he was too afraid he'd be noticed and eaten. The cry had been in him all this time, and he wanted desperately now to let it out. On that day, he cried out inside his own mind, "Momma! Momma! Don't leave me. I will die without you." Something inside him did die the day his mother was taken. But now, in this moment, he was fully alive again. In pain, but fully alive. He counted the wood he was touching among the most beautiful objects he had ever encountered. Actually, it was singularly beautiful. Like nothing he had seen or felt before. Now, for the first time since he was a pinky, he remembered his mother's face. That he had forgotten what she looked like had always been a source of great sadness for him. He remembered the hawk's cruel talons. Why couldn't he remember his own mother?

But now her face was before the eyes of his heart clear as if she had been standing there. She was a beautiful golden-gray, something like the reflection he sees in the drinking pond back home, but with a hint of red highlight. And he remembered her voice and the little reminder she would whisper to each one of them as she tucked them in beneath their oak leaves. *Sleep now, you have all you need: a field of stars above you, a world of dreams within you, and me to always love you.*

Billowtail's brothers and sisters perished after his mother's death. His aunt wouldn't take on more than one. While she wanted to preserve her family genes, one was sufficient for that. But she wouldn't take the risk of the extra mouths to feed, which might have ended up costing her some nutrition. He begged his aunt to save his brother and two sisters, but she wouldn't hear of it. "It's a matter of survival, dear," she had said. "When you grow up, you will understand." And, truth be told, he did. For a long time, he did. But now, after coming this far, after all that had happened, after Flora and the bridge and the cat and the eagle and the man in the brown robe, he didn't understand anymore.

CHAPTER FIFTEEN

THE NARROW ROAD

THE HAZELHARP ALLIANCE was relieved to find Billowtail, but not overly pleased with him. They stayed in Liébana so long, looking for him, that they lost the boy's trail.

Fortunately, Sugarcoat remembered that the boy, while in Burgos, had talked with his travel companions about his next two destinations: Liébana and the Cathedral of San Salvador in Oviedo. These two places apparently contain things that mean a great deal to the Great Pinkies and are well worth the detour off what is known as the French Way of getting to St. James' tomb in Compostela. "It is said that he who visits St. James, but not San Salvador, visits the servant but not the lord," the boy told the fellow pilgrims. And so The Alliance figured the boy was on his way there.

Sugarcoat did not always remember where she put things, but she was gifted with a precise memory for whatever she heard. One would have assumed it was the magic thread that had instilled in her this ability, but she had actually been quite astute, all her life, at remembering things in her own Squirrelish tongue. Anyway, it was this gift that allowed her, even after the thread was gone, to recount to The Alliance, word for word, the things she had heard earlier in the journey as the boy quoted from the Codex Calixtinus, the travel guide for pilgrims on the way to St. James' Cathedral in Compostela:

The pilgrim route is a very good thing, but it is narrow. For the road which leads us to life is narrow; on the other hand, the road which leads to death is broad and spacious. The pilgrim route is for those who are good: it is the lack of vices, the thwarting of the body, the increase of virtues, pardon for sins, sorrow for the penitent, the road of the righteous, love of the saints, faith in the resurrection and the reward of the blessed, a separation from hell, the protection of the heavens. It takes us away from luscious foods, it makes gluttonous fatness vanish ... constrains the appetites of the flesh which attack the fortress of the soul, cleanses the spirit, leads us to contemplation, humbles the haughty, raises up the lowly, loves poverty. It hates the reproach of those fuelled by greed. It loves, on the other hand, the person who gives to the poor. It rewards those who live simply and do good works.

The Codex, written by travelers who had already completed the journey, also contained practical advice. Apparently, the road is just as dangerous for Great Pinkies as it is for squirrels. It can also be a treacherous place for a horse, as one of the Codex excerpts confirms:

At a place called Lorca, to the east, flows the river known as the Salt Stream. Be careful not to drink it or water your horse there, because the river is lethal. On its banks, as we were going to San-

tiago, we found two Navarrese sitting there, sharpening their knives, waiting to skin the horses of pilgrims which die after drinking the water. When we asked, they lied and said the water was safe to drink. So we watered our horses, and two died at once, which the men then skinned.

Billowtail wondered why Sugarcoat decided to tell this story now, with the state of mind everyone was in. It was so morbid to think of someone being poisoned and then skinned.

"Caaaaw," a bird called from his perch above the road.

"I have to say," said Sir Sniff, nodding knowingly, while looking up into the trees. "I couldn't agree more, my feathered friend."

Sugarcoat smiled at Sir Sniff in the first light moments that had passed among the squirrels in many days.

"Well, I too very much agree with the Codex on its various topics," said Sugarcoat. "The broad road and the narrow road, et cetera."

The squirrels looked at her with skeptical eyes wondering how she could possibly agree with something so puzzling.

"Also, about the vanishing, gluttonous fatness," Sir Sniff added. He turned sideways and rubbed his paw over his belly from top to bottom, presumably to demonstrate its leanness. It was true that all of the squirrels' food intake had dramatically decreased. A squirrel can normally eat the equivalent of his own body weight in a week. And they had been lucky to get one good meal per day on this journey. But, strangely enough, none of their fatness had disappeared.

Unlike the lean times behind, this particular leg of the route provided ample food. The cork oaks bore the most tasty acorns the squirrels had ever tasted. It seemed they stopped to eat much more often than usual. Perhaps it was because they

were on no particular schedule. There was plenty
of time to look for food, since they were not following anyone and they didn't know exactly where
they were going. All of the squirrels ate heartily
except for Billowtail, who hadn't yet regained his
appetite. It wasn't just the loss of Tippy and the
magic thread, but now they had also lost the boy
because Billowtail was hiding in his corner in the
alcove of that peaceful place. He would still be
there, if a gray-robed man, sweeping up, hadn't
found him, let out a gasp, and shooed him out of
the place with his broom. Billowtail ran right out
the door, right into Izzy Twiggens.

"Billowtail, my lad! They're looking for ya.
They're all beside themselves with worry. You best
let me take you to them now."

"Please don't turn me in, Mr. Twiggens. I just
want to disappear. I beg you to just pretend you
never saw me."

"Ah, nonsense, lad. Remember what I told you.
You can stand against this thing. You've got an inner strength. I can see it right through that thick
golden pelt of yours."

Billowtail didn't feel strong inside or out. And
he certainly didn't feel golden. Though Sugarcoat,
Sir Sniff and Nip were all happy to see him when
he finally consented to being found, he knew he
was nothing but a liability to them. And every
step along the road to (hopefully) Oviedo was a reminder of that. They left Liébana the opposite way
they came, assuming that's what the boy would
have done, but there was a chance—a pretty good
chance actually—that they would never find him.

It would not be easy to determine the exact
route to Oviedo. They did not have a map, and
even if they did, rodents are not good at reading
maps. They also do not read signs, if there even
happens to be one. So, they were at the mercy of
sheer chance or luck or coincidence or fate, or

whatever you want to call it.

Without the magic thread, there was no way of overhearing where anyone was going. Though, if someone happened to mention the name Oviedo, they would recognize it. That appeared to be their only hope. So when they came across a large group of pilgrims, they decided to climb a large tree, take a rest and listen to the Great Pinkies' chatter. Nip hugged onto the trunk upside down. Billowtail rested on a horizontal branch. Sir Sniff sat in a lounging position on the crook where the branch met the trunk, chewing on a blade of grass, which hung from his mouth. And Sugarcoat, in the habit of getting in close to conversation, took her spot behind some bushes at the base of the tree. It was difficult for Sir Sniff, Billowtail and Nip, who were not accustomed to trying to decipher words. None of them heard "O"-anything in the hours they waited and listened.

And then, there it was! Billowtail heard it, but he was too afraid to say he had heard anything, for fear that he may be wrong and cause The Alliance even more trouble. So he remained quiet as he watched the young man who said it depart. And all the squirrels waited longer. Listening, waiting, listening, waiting. It was Nip, about an hour later, who finally attested to hearing it, and so The Alliance set out, following the pilgrim who said it. He was a large, round fellow, much older than the others, but a shell hung from his walking stick, just like the boy's and all the other pilgrims. A blackbird was the man's travelling companion. The bird perched on his shoulder and listened intently to the running commentary, most likely about the weather and the fauna, the wildlife, and the things he had seen on the Way.

The man slept very little, but when he did, a most thunderous noise escaped from his mouth. Or maybe it was his nose. The loudest blast came forth just before he would awaken – always long before dawn. It must have been loud enough to keep his own self awake. Since the man seemed to lack the ability to sleep 'til morning, he would light a candle and tell stories to his bird in the middle of the night. Sometimes his bird would even awaken and listen.

After a number of days, the man and his bird eventually and unknowingly led The Alliance to another building made of stone, which contained a large box. On the box was a carving of a man sitting on a throne with six men on one side of him and six on the other.

"That must be the treasure box of which the boy spoke," whispered Sugarcoat to her fellow squirrels, who had found a hiding spot inside a tiny dark room and were peeking out its door into a grander room.

"A treasure box?" Nip whispered. "Like the ones at the market? Filled with all the things that glitter?"

"In a way," Sugarcoat said. "But the things inside that box there are not at all shiny. There is, for example, an old rumpled cloth stained with blood, a clay pot and a very, very old piece of bread."

"I did not think humans would consider any of those things treasures," said Nip. "Why do they keep them in such a special box?"

"It is mystifying," said Sugarcoat. "But they all have to do with something that happened more than a thousand years ago. The clay pot held water at a wedding feast. The bread was broken and shared at a supper just before someone very important died."

"So it reminds them of him," Nip said.

"Something more than that," said Sugarcoat.

"What?" asked Billowtail. "What more than that?"

"I'm not sure," Sugarcoat answered. "But something."

"And why are they all so fascinated with the soiled cloth?" Billowtail asked.

"Maybe it has magic powers like the thread," Nip said. Billowtail felt a pain shoot through his stomach. He hated the mention of the thread.

"If I remember correctly what the boy said," replied Sugarcoat, "the cloth was used to cover the face of a friend who died to save them."

"In a war?"

"I do not think so. Not exactly."

"What do you mean not exactly?" Sir Sniff questioned.

"Well, I did hear him speak of the great battle, but it did not seem to be a typical war, as he said this friend laid down his life for the enemy as well."

"So he was defeated by the enemy?" asked Sir Sniff.

"No, he died but was not defeated." Sugarcoat became suddenly still and cocked her head. "Shhh. Look. Someone is coming."

The squirrels saw a Great Pinky dressed in a white garment, as white as white can get, coming right for the little room. One leg seemed to be a bit shorter than the other because his feet landed with an uneven shuffle. *Spiff-squeef, spiff-squeef, spiff-squeef.* The squirrels scattered each to a corner and made themselves as skinny as possible, so as not to be seen. One extra *spiff-squeef* and the man had past them by, fortunately, and entered in the adjacent door. They heard rustling as if he was settling himself in a chair and then a clearing of his throat. It was easy to hear him, not as if the noises were coming through a thick wall, but as if he were right in the same room. Billowtail realized there was a hole cut in the wall with a dark veil over it. It was impossible to see the man, but Billowtail had a sense his face was right there at the veil. More footsteps approached and the squirrels pressed their backs tighter into the corners and held their breath. This time, they were not so lucky.

The footsteps stopped and a shadow darkened the door and in stepped a Great Pinky. He said some words, and then some words came from the other side of the veil. Then the man touched his hand to his head, his chest and both shoulders, just like the Great Pinkies who loved the wood. When he opened the door and left, four squirrels scurried out with him, one of them cutting his trajectory so close to the man's ankle, she nearly tripped him. Billowtail, Nip, Sir Sniff and Sugarcoat did not wait long enough to read the expression on the man's face, but they did hear a number of gasps as they darted from the building.

They were unaware they were dashing right into a road and something large and heavy was making its way toward them. Fortunately, squirrels are among the fastest-thinking and most nimble members of the animal kingdom, and in lieu of being squashed by whatever it was, they leapt. Sugarcoat and Sir Sniff each found themselves on a spoke of a large wheel, turning round and round until their heads felt they would pop. Nip lay lengthwise on an axle and hugged it with his hands and feet, making himself as flat as possible so he wouldn't be crushed against the top of the wagon as the axle turned. Billowtail's landing was the least graceful of all. He was hanging by his hands from a beam under the cart, and had to keep his feet raised to keep them from scraping the ground.

Where they were headed was anybody's guess, but the torturous ride made walking seem not so bad anymore.

Billowtail drew his knees in and lifted his feet even higher to avoid a sizable rock in the road. "Oh, let this end soon!" Why he felt the need to force the words out is anybody's guess since saying them required a great deal of effort due to the shortage of breath caused from hanging with extended arms.

If the ride didn't end soon, the squirrels would be leaving behind Oviedo and all hope of finding Puttermunch.

CHAPTER SIXTEEN

THE CORONATION

W HO WOULD HAVE BELIEVED good fortune could be so good? When the cart finally came to a halt and all the squirrels
hastened to disembark and scamper to the nearest
shrub, they realized they had been hitching a ride
right under Puttermunch! They hadn't recognized
it from underneath, but it was Puttermunch's
cart. The boy had brought it to a stop to adjust his
pouch strap, pushing it back up on his shoulder.
Then he was off again, atop Gimblerigg, who was
pulling the cart and unwittingly leading a trail of
squirrels behind.

Several uneventful days and nights passed
wherein the squirrels did nothing but walk, jog,
eat and sleep. It was Nip's job to watch the cart
for all his waking hours, making sure to let everyone know if the cat ever left it. She never did. The

horse and the boy seemed to be getting as tired as the squirrels. Their pace had slowed. Everyone was hungry, as they were burning many more calories than they had time to consume in the short amounts of time the boy stopped to eat. Great Pinkies can take in nourishment rather quickly compared to squirrels. The massive amounts of traveling just didn't allow time to harvest, shell, and consume enough acorns.

Finally, they arrived at the outskirts of another town. Since the boy passed up the perfect dining spot for squirrels in favor of entering the city to find food fit for human consumption, it was decided that Sugarcoat would stay and keep an eye on him and the cart, while the others doubled back to the cluster of oaks to eat their fill. They gathered a pile for Sugarcoat to dine on when she joined them. They were expecting her to be quite happy, but she arrived so distraught, she didn't even notice the generous nut stash.

"I have some bad news," she said.

"No," Nip said, looking up from his nibbling. "No more bad news."

"The cat and kittens have been dispersed."

"What?" Sir Sniff asked. "What do you mean dispersed?"

"The boy gave the man the cats, and the man gave him some shiny round objects."

"Like at the fair in Pamplona."

"Yes, like that."

Unfamiliar with cats and their role in human lives, the squirrels, of course, did not know that the wretched beasts were valuable to humans for ridding the premises of mice, and that certain breeds were highly valued for their expert mousing skills and would fetch a fair amount of money at market.

"Looks like cat pottage is on the menu for someone tonight," said Sir Sniff.

"What about Puttermunch?" Billowtail asked.

"I was able to get into the cart, but there was no Puttermunch inside," Sugarcoat said. "Just the nauseating smell of cat."

"But where is he?" Billowtail lamented.

"There's no way of knowing," Sugarcoat said. "But he would be on solid food by now. He'd have no need to nurse."

"Will he know how to survive?" Billowtail asked. "Will he know how to be a regular squirrel?"

"I hope so," said Sugarcoat.

"So, what now?" Billowtail asked. "How on earth will we find him?"

"Maybe the boy will keep him," said Sir Sniff. "Which brings up a good point. Where is the boy now? Shouldn't we continue to track him? In case Puttermunch stays with him?"

"The boy is having a meal," Sugarcoat said. "He should be there a while."

"Oh, where could Puttermunch be?" Billowtail felt himself slipping into a panic. He looked up into the sky, which usually calmed him, but did nothing at the moment. "Where are you Puttermunch?"

"No way of knowing now," said Sugarcoat. "He could be anywhere in the world."

Billowtail exhaled heavily. "This is all my fault. If only I hadn't messed things up back in Liébana, we could have had Puttermunch by now and been on our way home."

"Silence, Billowtail," said Sir Sniff, gruffly. "We'll have no more of that now. We have whatever lies before us, and nothing of what lies behind, so let's cast our eyes ahead."

Billowtail wanted to argue, but there was really nothing to argue with. He could look behind him until time runs out, but his eyes would never see a change in even a single second of what had past.

"I think our only hope now is to think like a young squirrel," said Sir Sniff, "and try to imagine where he might go."

"I wish Tippy were here," said Nip.

Billowtail felt that all-too-familiar sting in his eyes and found a place on a log to sit away from the others.

"Do you think the boy would have let Puttermunch go free?" Nip asked.

"I don't know," said Sir Sniff. "The question is, did he think of him as a pet?"

"It's hard to say," said Sugarcoat. "I do not think he would have considered him a food source."

"Oh, good gracious," said Billowtail, burying his face in his paws.

"No," said Sir Sniff. "The boy does not seem like a savage."

"Well, he wouldn't have to be savage," said Sugarcoat. "Just hungry. I've seen you bite the head off a baby bird or two when you need sustenance."

"Let's leave my eating habits out of it, shall we?"

"I think we should return to the place where the cat was exchanged for the shiny objects and look for Puttermunch there," said Billowtail.

"Anyway," Sir Sniff pointed out, "it's not like I raised any of those baby birds, is it?"

"Puttermunch might be there trying to get back to the cat, since she is the only mother he probably has memory of," Billowtail interjected.

"And what about your frequent feasts on eggs, stolen right from the nest?" Sugarcoat countered.

"That's different."

"How is that different?"

"I think we should get moving as soon as possible," Billowtail persisted. "The more time that goes by, the bigger chance Puttermunch might move locations."

"I am merely pointing out that we are all part of a big chain," Sugarcoat said. "And we can't assume that somebody would never be another's supper."

"You are quite the cynic, Madame," said Sir Sniff. "Anyway, a creature Puttermunch's size would not make much of a meal, so I am going to presume he is up in a tree somewhere, exploring heretofore unexplored branches and sampling previously untasted nuts. Or perhaps making himself at home in someone's garden. I am a little envious of the little fellow, having seen so much of the world already. Who knew the delicacies available to squirrels? When this is all over, and Puttermunch is safe again at home, I may decide to retire near a vegetable garden."

"Pardon me for my boldness, Sir, but how can you be thinking of your own future at a time like this?" Billowtail asked.

Nip took a step back, away from Billowtail, as if to avoid being struck by whatever was going to strike.

"Is that not what you were doing, cowering in the corner of the Cathedral for those many hours?" Sugarcoat snapped. "Watch your tongue, boy! Where did you get the idea you could address an elder like that?"

"It's OK, Sugarcoat," said Sir Sniff. "The boy has a point. I am daydreaming a bit at a less than ideal time, I suppose. But I did say *after* we find Puttermunch."

"Well, if we don't go now, we aren't going to ever find Puttermunch," Nip chimed in. "And I want to go home. I am tired of the road. I don't care how many vineyards and gardens and exotic trees it has to offer. I want my old tree in Bon Arbre, and at this point, I have my doubts that I will ever see it again."

"Aw, I know it looks hopeless right now, kid, but you will be home before you know it," said Sir Sniff. "But, your point is well taken, and we best move out if we are going to locate Puttermunch."

The Alliance set out to the village where the

cats were sold. They searched tree, fountain, stream and stump, finding all kinds of squirrels, but not Puttermunch. And not any that had seen Puttermunch.

Camp was made that night in a barn, mostly because Nip had never been inside a barn before and was craving a new experience.

He tried to say good evening to the cow, but she just stared and then dropped her head to the ground and pretended to be using her wide nose to sift through the sand for grain.

Just as Billowtail was settling into the straw and finding that heavy and comfortable place behind his eyelids, Sugarcoat shot straight up out of her makeshift nest. "León!" she cried. "Of course, of course, of course. We are in León!"

"What?!!" Nip jumped up out of his hay bed. "Whu-, whu-, whu- what's going on? What happened Sugarcoat?"

"I just realized, this is the place the boy spoke of to the girl who fixed his leg. He told her all about the church that has become the resting place for royalty. And that's why the boy was looking at those tombs in that church today. We are in León!"

Billowtail wanted to join in her excitement, but he didn't know exactly why he should be excited.

"What significance does this have, Sugarcoat?" Sir Sniff said, speaking a bit slower than usual, due to his sleepiness. "How will this help us find Puttermunch?"

"I don't know," Sugarcoat said. "I am just relieved to know where we are."

"So we are in León," said Billowtail.

"Yes!" said Sugarcoat. "León!"

"And where is León?" asked Billowtail.

"León is in—well, you know. León is in—León. That's where León is."

"Wow," said Nip, with genuine wonder in his voice. "León."

THE CORONATION

One of the worst things in the world for a squirrel is to be lost. It was especially hard for a squirrel like Sugarcoat. It is difficult to be in control of things when you have no idea where you are.

Fortunately for Sugarcoat, the boy dashed his shin on a rock after leaving Logroño, stepping in a pothole which threw him off balance and sent him to the ground. He sought medical treatment at Santo Domingo de la Calzada, at the hospital set up for pilgrims on the way to Compostela. A beautiful young girl tended to the boy. She was the doctor's daughter, who helped nurse sick and injured pilgrims.

"The boy told the girl of many of the places he was bound," Sugarcoat told the squirrels, "including a place in León called the Basilica de San Isidoro, which started as a simple monastery, built in the 960s by order of King Sancho the Fat."

"See?" said Sir Sniff, proudly rubbing his furry round belly. "The Great Pinkies take fatness as a compliment or they wouldn't have given that title to their king."

Sugarcoat raised an eyebrow at Sir Sniff. "Anyway, that monastery was destroyed by invaders three decades after it was built. It was ordered to be rebuilt again seventy years later by Ferdinand I and was designated as the pantheon of kings.

"A pantheon? Sounds like a venomous snake," Nip observed.

"That's exactly what the nurse girl said!" Sugarcoat marveled. "But the boy told her it was a place where all the kings were buried."

"All the kings of the world?" Nip asked.

"I don't know. He just said, 'all the kings.' But it couldn't be *all* the kings because I heard the boy talk, on another occasion, of a king that was buried in Jerusalem."

"Where is that?"

"I don't know. But I get the feeling it is no ordinary place. The odd thing, I guess, is that the king is no longer buried there. The tomb is empty. It was discovered that the stone was rolled away three days after the king died, even though it was guarded, and mysteriously, there was no body inside."

"Hmmm," said Sir Sniff. "Odd indeed."

"Why are there no squirrel kings?" Nip asked.

"I don't know," said Billowtail.

"Wouldn't it be grand?" Nip said with a dreamy look in his eye.

"There is no squirrel king because there are no squirrel societies," said Sugarcoat. "People follow their kings. Squirrels don't follow. And they don't lead. They are alone."

"But *we* are not alone," said Nip. "We lead, and we follow."

"The Hazelharp Alliance is different. And very difficult. It's a difficult problem for us that we have to do these things. And only because we must find Puttermunch."

"But don't you think we need a king?" Nip asked. "Maybe if we had a king, we wouldn't get into so much trouble. Maybe we would be better squirrels if we had a king. Maybe Bon Arbre would be a better place."

"I never thought I would hear you admit that Bon Arbre could get any better," Billowtail said.

"A benevolent king," Sir Sniff mused. "But how to convince the citizens of Bon Arbre that they need a king? Will they not have difficulty understanding? Would we have understood were it not for the road?"

"They can be convinced," Nip said. "Squirrels are reasonable creatures."

"Reasonable?" Sugarcoat said. "Are you certain of this?" She was, no doubt, thinking of the life-long judgment and, on occasion, near condemnation she had received for being without color.

"Would anyone have been able to convince you to follow a king before this journey?"

"The road has changed us in a lot of ways," Nip agreed.

"The road is cruel," said Billowtail softly.

"The road stretches out before us and stretches behind," said Sugarcoat. "We must keep our feet moving all in one direction. The other is for our eyes only and even then only in quick glances, not in long, lingering stares."

With that, Nip emitted a large yawn, and Sir Sniff noticed the late hour. "We better get some sleep," Sir Sniff said. "There's no telling where the road will lead us tomorrow."

According to the account she would later give to The Alliance, Sugarcoat awoke long before everyone else and set about making a cape by gnawing through a feed sack and removing a swatch large enough to fit around her shoulders and touch the ground. She was quite pleased with her workmanship as the edges had hardly frayed at all. Then she crept out of the barn and found the youngest and most malleable limb on a nearby thorn bush, carefully gnawed off the emerging thorns and twisted it into a ring. She tried it on to make sure it was the proper size for a squirrel's head. She removed it and re-tied it a little looser. She gnawed at a few more areas that were still a bit scratchy. For a staff, she procured the smoothest, straightest stick she could find and then gave it additional smoothness by spitting on it and rubbing it with a small rough rock. She found a buttercup wildflower in a patch growing as a fringe around the barn and wedged the stem into a loose portion of the bark near the top of the staff. She wished she could find purple, the color of royalty, but the little yellow flower would have to do for now, since everyone would be waking soon. She hoped they would accept the decision she had made. Nip's idea was inspired. The

Alliance surely needed royalty.

The rooster awoke first, of course, and announced his raspy approval of the sunrise. Then, the chickens, cows, sheep and horses awoke, followed by three squirrels, blinking and stretching at the orange hues of dawn.

Sugarcoat called all the animals to attention.

"Citizens of León and travelers who hail from far away," she addressed them regally. "It is my great pleasure to present to you, on the occasion of this Royal Coronation, a new King." She unfurled the folded feedbag cape and approached Sir Sniff.

The animals stood in speechless awe as she placed the cape around his shoulders. Then she retrieved the thorn bush crown and buttercup scepter from behind a bale of hay. Sir Sniff bowed his head for easier placement of the crown and took the scepter in his wide hand.

Sugarcoat gave a profound curtsy and an official introduction: "Hail, hail, all hail, Sir Sniff, king of The Hazelharp Alliance, ruler of the Way, benevolent King of Bon Arbre."

Billowtail and Nip bowed in unison and all the farm animals lowered their heads. A shaft of sunlight pierced into the barn and illuminated Sir Sniff from behind, casting a dream-like glow around him, so his fur looked tinged with orange embers.

"This is a great honor," said Sir Sniff. "A great honor indeed. I am not exactly sure what a king is supposed to do, but I will try my best not to let any of you down."

"You know, like Flickertail, the Chipmunk King," said Nip. "A king is supposed to tell everyone what to do."

"I thought that was Sugarcoat's job," said Sir Sniff with a wide smile.

"Actually, it's much more than that," said Sugarcoat. "A king is charged with protecting his subjects—with putting their welfare before his own."

"Someone get Billowtail a reed," said Nip. "Play for us Billowtail!"

"Oh, I can't—I don't—I don't even remember how to play, it's been so long."

"Oh, please Billowtail!" Nip begged.

"Every coronation needs music," coaxed Sugarcoat.

"I could order it done," Sir Sniff boomed. "No minstrel would dare disregard the king's wishes."

All the squirrels looked at their new king, half shocked and half dismayed.

"No, no," he said, with a smile. "I am just playing with you. I would not abuse my power." He put his arm around Billowtail. "But it would be nice to hear you play on this momentous occasion."

And so, because Billowtail couldn't say no to a friend who wanted to hear music, he played for his king. And they all danced—the squirrels and the chickens, anyway. Even the cow, though large animals normally do not have any sense of rhythm, managed a slight nod of the head on each downbeat.

CHAPTER SEVENTEEN

THE DEAD FOREST

IT WAS DECIDED THAT they should continue to follow the boy in case, by chance, Puttermunch had returned to the only home he knew—the cart where he was nursed. Maybe the boy had decided to keep Puttermunch. Maybe they had grown attached to one another. There were nursery rhymes and legends which spoke of Great Pinkies and squirrels becoming friends, and most everyone supposed it could happen in real life. Even Sugarcoat declined to discount the possibility, especially after having her life saved by a man in a brown robe.

The next leg of the journey started out uneventful and dull, so the squirrels were actually happy to see that the boy had decided to cross a creek. Not that they liked to swim, necessarily, because squirrels don't often choose it as sport, though they are very good at it should the need arise. But

The Alliance welcomed it now as something different, since they had seen the same sameness for so many days.

Once on the other side, their hearts sank. The trudge was about to become even more uninspiring than it had been on the other side of the creek. Opening up before them was an expanse of branchless black tree trunks, stretching across a barren floor as far as the eye could see.

"Eerie," said Nip.

"What happened to this place?" asked Billowtail.

"Fire," said Sir Sniff solemnly.

"Fire?"

It seemed to Billowtail that the boy and his horse were the only other living things within miles. There was no chirping of birds. No buzzing of insects. Everything was charred black and hopeless. Nobody could have predicted when they entered this desolation that it would go on for so many endless acres. The squirrels began to theorize that the boy was lost, had taken a wrong turn somewhere along the line and was possibly leading them in circles. Very, very large circles.

Since leaving Bon Arbre, Billowtail had found the times without trees the most trying. The ground was the least efficient way to travel. Swinging from tree to tree the most. There was also the inability to fall asleep and stay asleep without benefit of the swaying branches, grown to a height tall enough to protect from predators. And the inability, of course, to harvest nuts and seeds. But it wasn't just the physical trials of a squirrel being treeless, which were trials enough. Added to all of this was the emotional difficulty. No one can know what that is like for a squirrel. Even most other squirrels don't know and can't possibly begin to imagine since they are never without their trees, except on rare occasion when a migration is in order and that's nothing that has happened in Billowtail's lifetime, nor even Sir Sniff's.

So depression set in for the squirrels of The Alliance, but most particularly for Billowtail, who of course was still grieving his role in Tippy's loss. Once a squirrel gets in this dismal state of mind, it is difficult enough to escape. But take trees out of his life and it is nearly impossible.

Among all his siblings, why did it have to be him who survived, Billowtail wondered. Why couldn't it have been someone who would not make such a mess of things?

The boy walked until evening fell, and then curled up in his cart under a blanket. The squirrels found an abandoned tunnel, carved by a society of underground creatures of similar size to the squirrels. When it was time, they could sleep there. It was close to the cart, so they could hear what the boy was up to, and it would provide protection from predators, if there did happen to be any living things left in this forsaken wasteland.

Sugarcoat looked worried.

"What is it, Sugarcoat?" asked Sir Sniff, who is not one to let worry go unmentioned. "What distresses you?"

"Food has been scarce the last few days. All who travel this route must be very hungry. Including the boy."

"Why does this concern us?" Billowtail asked, drawing parallel lines in the dust with his toenails.

"Remember what happens when we are short of our preferred food," Sugarcoat said.

"What?" asked Nip, drawing perpendicular lines to Billowtail's parallel ones.

"We nut and bark eaters get desperate enough to start robbing nests," Sugarcoat said.

"So?" Nip said. "Why should we care if the boy eats eggs and birds."

"The boy doesn't need to look for nests. He has

food right in his hands."

"Oh, I wish you wouldn't bring this up again," said Billowtail.

"I thought you said humans don't eat their animal friends," Nip said. "He hasn't eaten his horse, and a horse would make a much heartier meal than a baby squirrel."

"He needs his horse for transportation," Sugarcoat said.

"What about the kittens?" Nip said. "He didn't eat any of them. Even when he was without food for awhile."

"How do you know?" Sugarcoat said.

"Well because—uh—oh, I don't know for sure."

"Kittens are domesticated animals," Sir Sniff said. "Great Pinkies are not likely to eat pets. They consider them companions, not food."

"But squirrels," Billowtail gulped and felt nausea overtake him. "Squirrels are wild animals."

"But he has raised Puttermunch," Nip said. "Wouldn't that make him a pet?"

"I don't know," said Sugarcoat. "Maybe not if he were hungry enough."

"We don't even know if he still has Puttermunch," Sir Sniff reminded.

"Well, that brings us to another topic," Sugarcoat said. "How are we going to find out? I am beginning to question the wisdom in continuing to pursue a cart that may very well be lacking a baby squirrel. Meanwhile, Puttermunch could be out there somewhere in grave danger or just slipping farther and farther away from us."

"Well, I could—"

"Eh, eh, Billowtail," Sugarcoat said firmly. "Don't get any ideas. You must learn from your mistakes if you are to grow."

"What do you mean? You haven't let me finish, I was just going to say that I—"

"Eh, eh, there you go again. You mustn't start

any sentence with 'I' when it comes to rescuing Puttermunch."

"We?"

"Yes, Billowtail. You must think in terms of 'we,' not 'I.' This is what we all have learned. The hard way."

"The very, very hard way," Nip agreed, hanging his head.

"I'm sorry, Nip," Billowtail said. "I'm really sorry. I know nothing is going to be the same for you without Tippy. Or for me either. Nothing's going to be the same for any of us."

"Now you've got it, Billowtail," Sugarcoat said, laying a paw on his shoulder. "Us."

"Us?"

"It's not about you, or me, or I, or you, or he, or she. It's about us."

"'Us' hurts a lot more," Billowtail said.

Sugarcoat's eyes softened. "You're right, Billowtail. It does."

"Then, why are we doing it?"

"Because there is no other way, Billowtail. If there was, believe me, I would be all for it. This doesn't come naturally to me either. You know me."

Yes, it was true. All squirrels are prone to thievery, but Sugarcoat had stolen more than her share of nuts from her neighbors, including Billowtail. Quite regularly, in fact. She has an extra keen sense of smell, maybe because she lacks acuity in her eyes, and is an expert at sniffing out someone else's stash. The other squirrels were also somewhat intimidated by her. If you had asked them why, they would have said it was because she is white, and they would have believed their own words. But it really had nothing to do with color. Sugarcoat would have been intimidating in any color.

Since The Alliance formed, intimidation had

been overshadowed, or maybe even replaced, by respect. Billowtail had seen Sugarcoat put aside her own desires for someone else's sake. And that is why he gladly followed her. And that is why he took her criticisms and admonishing to heart. As much as they were unreserved, they were also not undeserved.

"So, what is our plan?" Billowtail asked. "How will we find out if the boy still has Puttermunch?"

"Well, now that the cat's gone, what's keeping us from sneaking into the cart?" Nip asked.

"A hungry boy with a bow and arrow?" Sir Sniff said.

"Don't forget," Sugarcoat said. "Puttermunch may or may not be a pet to him. But *we* certainly fall into the category of supper. We best wait until Puttermunch ventures away from the cart."

"Or one of us could sneak in," suggested Nip, "while the rest of us stand as sentinels ready to—"

"Shhhh," hissed Sugarcoat. "Do you hear that?"

A faint scuffing of dead leaves wafted on the still evening air.

"Someone is coming," Sugarcoat whispered making it a point to make her eyes wide. "It's someone small, but bigger than we are. A quadruped."

Nip gasped. "What is that?"

"Someone who walks on four feet," Sir Sniff said.

"Is it coming our way, Sugarcoat?" Billowtail asked. "Do you think it can smell us?"

"Oh yes. And oh yes. Get in the tunnel!"

She ran for one of several holes that led into the underground dwelling and disappeared into the ground, followed by Nip, Billowtail and Sir Sniff. They huddled together at the bottom, and looking right and left, could see the tunnel was much more intricate than they had thought, and had a number of connected passageways, several of which led back up to ground level.

Now everyone heard the crunching of whatever feet were stepping on ashen devastation. The footsteps were not so subtle anymore and quite unsettling. Then it came on loud and clear and terrifying.

"What do we do?" Billowtail asked in an intense whisper.

Sugarcoat looked at Sir Sniff, whose composure never comes undone. He appeared close to entering a controlled panic. This Billowtail could see, even in the dark tunnel, because squirrels have excellent night vision. "Just be completely still," he whispered. "And no more talking after this word." His pointer finger shot up to his lips.

The scuttling got closer and closer until finally it stopped. Nip opened his mouth, and Sir Sniff grabbed him around the shoulders and placed his hand over his mouth, sealing the opening forcefully enough so that his paw was going to have tooth marks if and when he finally let go.

They all curled up together quietly for the next several heartbeats. Billowtail could hear his own heart pounding in his throat, and he might have even heard a few other heartbeats as well. That's how quiet it was in there and that's how closely packed they all were. There was really no room to breathe, and no desire to, anyway, for fear that breath might be heard, or the vibration of it might be felt or otherwise detected by whatever predator might find underground creatures tasty. They had heard horrific stories from the ground squirrels back home and actually even witnessed the brutal snatchings. And just as all of this was rushing through Billowtail's mind, a torrent of charred leaves and dry dirt crashed into a hole to the north and then came the sound of rocks chipping against each other above ground and then the same progression of events at the south entrance of the tunnel.

"Oh, no," Billowtail cried. "We're going to die."

"Silence, Billowtail!" Sugarcoat hissed. "You say something like that and you surely will."

"But it's blocking all our alternate exits," Billowtail insisted, "and it will be waiting for us at the only one that's left open. I've seen this done to ground squirrels back home."

Nip let out a small whimper followed by a desperate plea: "I don't want to be eaten."

"No, not all the exits could be blocked," Sugarcoat said. "I've been in ground squirrel dwellings before, you might remember, and there were quite a few connecting tunnels. We just have to find them. Come on, let's split up."

"Split up?" Billowtail was mortified, and quite unaware of the irony of his fear. All his adult life, he had accomplished everything without aid from another living being. Now being on his own was unthinkable, and he wondered how Sugarcoat could suggest it.

"Can't we stay together and look?" Nip squeaked.

"We'll begin together," Sugarcoat said, "but then we'll likely have to separate to branch off."

They slunk single file through the main tunnel, first Sugarcoat, then Billowtail, then Nip and Sir Sniff.

Dust filled the tunnel like smoke, making it difficult to breathe, although it might have been the anxiety too. They had entered into a place where there was no light whatsoever. Billowtail felt as if he were buried alive and would almost rather have gone up into open space and come face to face with whatever wanted to eat him.

"What is it?" Nip said, looking up as he walked, as if he might be able to see through the two feet of earth onto the ground above. "What's up there?"

"If you want my educated guess," said Sugarcoat, "it's a badger. His plans are to block all of our escape routes except one, then dig us out and eat us one by one."

"No," Nip whimpered. "I'm too young to be eaten."

The four moved through the tunnel as one, staying together by using the tail-to-cheek method, each squirrel's tail brushing the cheek of the squirrel behind him. But it wasn't long before a separation was necessary. They came to a kind of fork in the tunnel.

"Sir Sniff, you take Nip and go North. I'll go South, and Billowtail, you go east. Whoever finds a way out—"

Before Sugarcoat could finish her sentence, another debris fall could be heard, this time to the north and much farther away.

"So that's where he is," said Sir Sniff. "Well, at least now we know."

"But what if that was the last emergency exit?" Nip panicked.

"We can make a run for the main exit, where we came in, if we turn around now," said Billowtail.

"We'll never beat him back there and still have time to escape," Sir Sniff said. "He'll snatch us before we even get our heads out of the ground."

"What if we stay where he can't reach us?" Billowtail suggested.

"These are desperate times," Sugarcoat said. "He has no other choice of food. He will wait us out or dig us out. He will not go away hungry."

"Look, we have no time for discussion and debate," Sir Sniff said. "Everyone turn around!"

Billowtail was relieved the plan to separate had been scrapped. However petrifying what lay ahead might be, it was less petrifying than being alone.

The Alliance scurried and slunk back through the tunnel, this time with Sir Sniff in the lead, Nip following, then Billowtail and Sugarcoat, all still using the tail before them for guidance. Nip let out a small whimper with every step. It took all Billowtail had not to do the same.

"Nip," Sir Sniff whispered, with crisp conso-
nants, not turning or stopping. "You've got to try
to be quiet, in case it can hear us down here. It will
know where we are and meet us at the exit hole."

Nip let out one final whimper and then spent
the rest of the route blowing unintended bursts of
fear out his nose.

"Right here," Sir Sniff said and then began the
ascent up to ground level. Each squirrel beneath
got snouts and eyes full of small rocks and gravel
as the squirrel above momentarily lost and then
regained footing.

"I will exit on my own first," Sir Sniff whispered
as he strained against gravity. "If it is safe, the rest
of you can follow."

"No," Billowtail said, his feet scrambling to
move faster over the falling gravel. "I will go first."

"Don't be ridiculous," Sir Sniff said. "It's too
dangerous."

"I know it's dangerous," he said struggling
to find some traction with his feet. "That's why
I should go first. I am expendable. You have too
much wisdom. The Alliance can't afford to lose its
king."

"Nobody is expendable," Sir Sniff said.

"Fools are," Billowtail said.

"No," Sir Sniff said. "Not even fools."

Billowtail was glad to hear that, but he desperately wanted to redeem himself, so before he could
give it any more thought, he was climbing over Sir
Sniff, in an effort to be the first to reach ground
level. Sir Sniff tried to fight him back, and in the
scuffle, they both lost their footing on the vertical
wall of the tunnel and fell back down to the bottom
of the hole, taking Nip and Sugarcoat with them.
They landed in a pile, with Nip at the very bot
tom, then Sugarcoat and Sir Sniff stacked on top
of him, and Billowtail at the very top.

"Oh no!" Nip whined as he pulled himself out from under the wriggling pile of dirt-caked fur. "Now we have to start all over again. What if we don't make it up in time?"

While the rest of the squirrels struggled to pick themselves up, Billowtail wallowed on the ground, with his head in his paws. "I did it again," he said. "Trying to be a hero."

"Come on Billowtail," Sugarcoat pleaded, pulling on his arm, which had more stretch and give in it than any squirrel arm ought to. "You better get up. We're not going anywhere without you."

"You'd be better off," he said.

"Nonsense!" Sugarcoat said "You've done some foolish things, there's no denying that, but we would most certainly not be better off without you."

And then there was nothing left for discussion. A huge pointy mouth with razor-sharp teeth forced its way into the hole.

The four squirrels ducked into a fetal position and put their hands over their heads. A swipe of a paw followed, displaying claws as sharp as swords. Because the squirrels had all fallen to the bottom, the badger struck nothing but air and some dirt from the walls along the side of the hole. It began to dig frantically.

"Everybody run!" called Sir Sniff. "To the end of the tunnel!! We have to find another exit."

"How do you know they are not all plugged up?" Nip asked, wanting some kind of assurance of survival.

"I don't," said Sir Sniff. "But it is our only hope."

"Does being eaten hurt as bad as it looks?"

"Don't think like that, Nip," said Sugarcoat. "We have to get out of this alive. For Puttermunch. For Mrs. Poggins. And for ourselves."

The digging and scratching began to grow

louder, even as the squirrels believed they were getting farther away from the badger.

"He must be digging deeper and wider," Sir Sniff said.

"Bad news up here," Sugarcoat declared from the front of the line. "No exit."

"Let's keep moving," Sir Sniff directed.

"More bad news then," Sugarcoat replied. "There's no place else to move. We're at the end."

"It seems the badger is excavating this entire colony," said Sir Sniff.

"Which means," said Sugarcoat, "there soon will be no tunnel left to hide in."

Nip let out another involuntary whimper. Billowtail drew a shaky, elongated breath.

"Then, we won't hide," said Sir Sniff. "We'll wait for the badger to unearth us and then we'll make a run for it."

"How?" asked Billowtail. "He'll have us in his jaws the minute he digs us up."

"He can't catch all of us at once," Sir Sniff said.

"Right," said Sugarcoat. "We'll scatter to the four winds."

"Three," said Sir Sniff.

"Three?" Sugarcoat asked.

"One of us will certainly be prey to the beast," said Sir Sniff. "I will stay."

"No, Sir Sniff," Billowtail said.

"I am the oldest. I have lived my life."

"No." That's all Billowtail knew to say.

"Now Billowtail," said Sir Sniff. "Remember what happened last time you argued about this?"

"I saved us all."

"And quite by accident, my dear boy," Sir Sniff said. "You could have gotten us all killed."

"Like I did to poor Tippy. Please let me try to redeem myself. I want to go first."

"No, you don't," said Sir Sniff. "You want to end your suffering. But this is not the way. You will see your suffering end, but not like this. You have many great things to do still ahead. Many great things. My great things are in my past. Except for this one more."

The scratching and digging was louder and even more frantic now, and it was clear there was probably not thirty seconds left.

"But you are the king," said Billowtail. "Our king."

"A king protects his subjects," Sir Sniff reminded, "laying down his life if necessary."

Nip threw his arms around Sir Sniff and wept into his fur, coarse and caked with dirt. The mingled tears made mud on Nip's cheek. "I don't want you to—"

Sniff let his paws rest lightly on Nips shoulder. "Don't fret now, young one. I have a plan. And regardless of its success, you will go on beautifully."

"How?" Billowtail whispered, too soft for anyone to hear.

One final slicing of dirt and all were exposed to the ferocious fangs of the ravenous badger.

Sir Sniff pushed Nip hard, breaking the tight clasp he had around his midsection. "Run!" Sir Sniff yelled as he bolted straight for the badger, aiming for the opening between his legs, in hopes of leading him on a chase into the dark night. "Everybody run!"

Billowtail and Nip managed a split-second hesitation before Sugarcoat grabbed them each by a forearm and pulled so hard, they would later learn, she left claw marks.

As they ran, there was the awful sound of Sir Sniff's fight, his cries of pain and then finally silence except for the snapping of jaws.

"Just keep running," Sugarcoat said, prodding the two younger squirrels from behind. Don't look back."

As soon as she said it, Billowtail looked back,

but he could see nothing through the darkness.

"I said don't look back, Billowtail!"

He and Nip looked at each other with desperate sadness.

"It had to be what it is," said Sugarcoat as the three continued to run. "It had to be." Her voice cracked as she said it. They had never heard a crack in her voice before. And they would never have predicted they ever would have.

The three must have run a hundred acres before they came to a wide ravine. They crossed it and made a vertical ascent right up the first live tree they found. Billowtail rested on a branch, panting, and clutched a leaf in his fist. It felt cool and soft and comforting, unlike anything he had felt before, though he had seen and touched a hundred thousand leaves. The devastation was over and they had entered an area of lush vegetation.

"We will be able to eat here," said Sugarcoat softly.

Though it had been days since they'd had food, none of them were hungry.

"I won't be able to eat without Sir Sniff," said Nip. "He died hungry."

"You surely will too if you don't eat," said Sugarcoat. Her eyes were red and swollen. Another thing they never would have predicted.

"Come on," she said, pulling on an acorn. "We will need our strength. We must not forget our purpose and the reason our brave friends have given their lives. Puttermunch and Mrs. Poggins are counting on us."

"I don't see how it will be possible anymore," said Nip.

"Who would have thought any of us would lose our lives?" Billowtail said. "Life was much easier before this journey began. We thought we had our problems back in Bon Arbre. But everything was so simple then. We awoke in the morning to a new day, and all it brought was work and nourishment and occasionally a short spell of play, wrestling with a twig or rolling a pinecone downhill. It was much easier when we only had to take care of ourselves, when our lives were not mixed up with someone else's, and our hearts did not feel like they were being ripped from our chests. I want to go home, Sugarcoat."

"Now, Billowtail," Sugarcoat returned to her firm voice. "Despair is never becoming of a squirrel. Besides, we can't go back."

Billowtail remembered that awful moment that lay before him, when he will have to tell Mrs. Whimtucket about Tippy.

"You're right," Billowtail said. "Nothing but sorrow awaits us there."

"We can return home, Billowtail. Someday. But we can't go back the same way we came. The journey has changed us."

Billowtail looked deep into her eyes. "I didn't want to be changed. It hurts too much."

"You would have rather not known Sir Sniff and Tippy."

"I would have rather known them forever."

"Then you will have to endure the pain that is required of having known things that endure."

"How do you know all of this, Sugarcoat?" Nip asked, chewing a twig, more to release his nervousness than to extract nourishment. "You're just a tree squirrel like us, aren't you? Some folks back home say you have special powers. But my Momma told me there was no such thing."

"I am a tree squirrel just like you," she said softly. "But I have known other things for a while now."

"Other things? What other things?"

"Ever since the vineyard. There was something in his face, and I came to know something I've never known before."

"Something in whose face?"

"The one who saved me. Of course, I owe my life to you and Tippy. But I feel I owe something beyond life to him. Or rather to something I saw in his face."

Billowtail and Nip looked at each other, each with the realization that they might be losing Sugarcoat as well. Not in the way they lost Tippy and Sir Sniff. But in the way that happens to some squirrels when first they begin talking nonsense and then they can't stand on their two hind legs without falling over. Sometimes it happens after a blow to the head, and sometimes something gets inside of them and makes them sick.

"Have you forgotten?" asked Billowtail. "Have you forgotten what he did to Tippy?"

"Sometimes there is more than we can know, Billowtail."

Billowtail and Nip glanced at each other again, and if they could have read each other's minds, they would have realized they were both thinking that the two of them were about to be left to finish the journey on their own. Maybe it was something in the dead forest that entered Sugarcoat's brain and was killing it from within.

"Shhh," said Sugarcoat. "Someone's coming."

The squirrels fell silent, as three great pinkies approached on foot, their bags, bows and blankets strapped to them. The squirrels had been so relieved to see a live tree, none of them had noticed the footpath that ran the length of the ravine, as far as the eye could see, in both directions.

"Hey," Nip whispered, "we've seen them before."

One of them looked up into the tree.

Sugarcoat grabbed Nip's arm and placed her forefinger over her mouth, hoping he could read the warning in her intense eyes. She did not even dare to whisper her admonition to hold complete silence or become sustenance for the humans, who are bound to be as hungry as any other creature coming out of what seems like an endlessly-expansive dead forest, if indeed they had come from there.

The three men sat under the tree and opened their bags. The squirrels watched their heads bobbing back and forth as they got their food out and took swigs from canteens. The men were doing a fair amount of chattering over supper, and the squirrels were eating small bites of their own food because they knew they should, and slowly their hunger began to drive them as their bodies' deficits overtook their grief. The acorns—the first they'd seen in five days—tasted good.

Suddenly, Sugarcoat stopped chewing and cocked her head. "Shhhh, shhhh," she hissed, pointing her left ear down toward the Great Pinkies. "Compostela! They said it! They must be going our way!"

CHAPTER EIGHTEEN

FOOT DUST

H OW MUCH FARTHER?" Nip asked, as the trio of squirrels followed the trio of men through the most beautiful greenness they had seen in a long time.

"I told you before, Nip, there's no way of knowing," said Sugarcoat.

"It's just that this place reminds me so much of Bon Arbre," Nip said. "I miss it. I just want to find Puttermunch and go home."

Billowtail was lost in his thoughts about his feet and how much they had changed since the beginning of this journey. He could only vaguely recall the ache on the balls of his feet. The blisters were now calluses. He could probably walk across burning embers without flinching. The internal groanings and chronic grumblings and verbalized complaints about various discomforts of the road had subsided. They had been replaced. There were now only three states of mind: quiet acceptance, sheer terror, or profound grief.

"What if we get all the way to Compostela and the boy is not there?" Nip asked.

"We will think of that then," Sugarcoat said.

"Or what if he is there, but we can't find him?" the young squirrel persisted.

"We will think of that then."

"Or what if we find him, but he does not have Puttermunch? Then where will we look?"

"We will think of that then."

"Why not now?" Billowtail asked.

"We must stay faithful to the road we are on."

What if the road is leading us nowhere?" asked Billowtail.

"We have no other road to follow. So, we must follow it."

The three stayed close on the heels of the three pilgrims, sleeping when they slept, walking when they walked, stopping to eat and drink only when they stopped, always making sure to stay out of their line of sight since they were known consumers of small animals. The squirrels had watched them shoot and eat possums. But it was unclear how picky about their fare they may be. It is more than a sure bet that any animal with meat on its bones, regardless of how small, would be desirable to hungry travelers.

"Is there no way of knowing how far we are?" Nip persisted. "No way at all?"

"Well, there is this certainty," Sugarcoat replied. "We are closer now than we ever were before. And we will be closer come sunset than we were at sunrise."

"I miss Sir Sniff," Nip said.

Sugarcoat stopped in her tracks, turned and sprung, knocking Nip to the ground and pinning him there. Her eyes turned to slits. "Look, all you have been doing since we lost Sir Sniff is complaining that I am not good enough. Well, I am all that you have, so you will have to learn to accept it."

"I—I—I—am not complaining," Nip stammered.

"Uhm, please, you two, the Great Pinkies are getting away," said Billowtail, who was the only one to notice that the road ahead had bent and the men were no longer in view.

"You are doubting," Sugarcoat bellowed at Nip. "You must not doubt."

"Shhh. Maybe—maybe—maybe—" Billowtail panted and stammered, debating whether to pull Sugarcoat off of Nip or whether being touched would enrage her. "Maybe we should keep it down."

"The Alliance will crumble if you doubt," Sugarcoat yelled into Nip's face, "and all will be lost."

Nip turned his face to the side and began to weep.

Sugarcoat's eyes softened and she dropped her head. She got up and extended a paw to Nip. He hesitated and looked at Billowtail, who nodded approval at accepting Sugarcoat's offer.

"I am sorry, Nip," Sugarcoat said, helping him up. "I am sorry. The pressure is getting to me too, I suppose. I do not know what we are doing or what is next. I know Sir Sniff would know, but I do not. I miss him every bit as much as you do. And I am sorry. Again. I am sorry." She said all these things to the ground, but with heartfelt contrition.

"It's OK," Nip said, wiping his eyes. "It's OK. I am sorry to have been so bothersome."

"Now, let's go," said Sugarcoat, placing a paw on his shoulder. "Let's go forward."

They ran a short distance along the road. It wasn't long before they caught sight of the humans again, and they all walked on in silence until evening. They found a place on a high branch to make camp.

As the stars appeared, Sugarcoat was lulled to

sleep by the chirping of the crickets. Nip and Billowtail watched her sleep.

"Do you suppose she's got it bad?" Nip asked.

"I don't know," Billowtail said. "She makes so much sense sometimes."

"What if we aren't even on our way to Compostela? What if she never heard that word at all?"

"I don't know, Nip. I just don't know."

"The things she said about the Great Brown Pinky. How could she say those things after what he did to Tippy?"

Billowtail did not want to admit that he understood what she saw in the man's face. He had seen it before too, on the bridge. But calling on the eagle to snatch Tippy, was inexplicably cruel. Who could do such a thing to a poor, weak, sick creature?

"I don't know, Nip."

"What do we do, Billowtail?"

"We have only one choice right now. We follow this road. Like Sugarcoat said."

"And if she has lost her mind?"

"We still have no other choice. This road is our only hope."

"Hey!" A voice shot through the night from a neighboring tree. "What's all the twitter-chatter up there, so late at night?"

"Who's there?" Billowtail called over. "Who are you?"

The leaves of a branch about the same level as their own rustled, and a squirrel appeared. The soft moonlight glinted off her cream-colored face. She had a light cream underbelly as well, and a warm-brown marking that extended from the top of her head down her back, like a hooded cape. Billowtail felt some unexplainable relief at laying eyes on her. She was the most beautiful squirrel he had seen in all his life, but that wasn't it. It wasn't a relief for his eyes that she had caused. It was a relief to his heart.

"How, how long have you been there?" Billow-tail asked.

"You mean to ask, how much of your conversation did I hear?"

"Yes," said Billowtail. "That's what I mean to ask."

The stranger leapt from her branch to his and made a little bow before him. "I am Ivy Silkpocket."

"I am Billowtail." He made a slight bow of the head. "And this is Nip Timbersham."

"A pleasure to make your acquaintance," Nip said.

"The pleasure is mine, Mr. Timbersham," Ivy said, "and Mr. uh—"

"Just Billowtail."

"Is that your first or last name, sir?"

"My only name."

"And a fine name it is," she nodded. "Sounds regal."

"Nothing regal about me," said Billowtail, trying to remember what regal meant.

"So, what brings you to La Hermosa? It is not often that we have visits from tree squirrels. Actually, it's not ever."

"We are looking for a baby squirrel who fell into the saddlebag of a pilgrim on his way to Compostela," Billowtail said. "Have you heard of Compostela?"

"I have heard of faraway places, but not that one. Sorry. But how old is this baby squirrel?"

"Well, he would be—hmmm." Billowtail rubbed his chin, not that he had ever done that before and not that it really helps anyone to think more clearly, but he thought it would make him look more regal. Whatever that meant. "How old would Puttermunch be now?" he asked no one in particular.

"He would be much older," said Nip. Billowtail gazed at him. "Than he was then, I mean."

"Yes, well he was just a pinky when we started

our journey to find him," Billowtail explained to Ivy Silkpocket. "But I don't know how long we've been gone. Our king was the one keeping count of the days, and he—"

Billowtail couldn't bring himself to say it.

"Your king?" Ivy cocked her delicate head.

"What's going on here?" Sugarcoat had awoken and was rubbing her knee while blinking her eyes open fully. "Who is this?"

"This is Miss Ivy Silkpocket," Nip said.

"Nice to make your acquaintance," said Sugarcoat. "I hope we aren't causing you any trouble." Sugarcoat looked from Billowtail to Nip and then back again.

"Not at all. We were just discussing the little one. Seems I may have seen him come through here."

"What?!" Billowtail exclaimed. "When?!!"

"Don't know how many sunsets ago, but it wasn't very many. I found him an odd little fellow. He had a human companion. Humans can make nice pets, but they have minds of their own and they can turn on you."

"Turn on you?" Billowtail asked.

"Yeah, right about the time you get them trained to give you a nut when you run up their leg, they decide you'd make a nice supper."

"But the boy that was with Puttermunch. He didn't look hungry, did he?" Nip asked.

"No, not particularly."

"Which way did they go?" Billowtail pressed.

"Up yonder way." Ivy pointed down the road where The Alliance was bound come daybreak. "Don't ask me what's over there as I've never been."

"That's Compostela over that way," Sugarcoat informed. "Somewhere."

"It has to be him you saw," said Billowtail.

"The boy who had the squirrel, he had a walking stick. And on it was something I have seen a number of times before. Many of the Great Pinkies have them."

"What is it?" Billowtail asked.

"It is nothing from around here," Ivy said. "No one here could tell me what it was. I will show you one if you like."

"Of course," said Billowtail.

Ivy disappeared for a moment as Sugarcoat, Billowtail and Nip waited silently for her return, looking up at the stars, which were partially drowned out by the light of the waning moon. Ivy returned with a roundish sort of scalloped object the perfect size for a squirrel to collect acorns in, but Billowtail suspected it hadn't been used for something so ordinary.

"I have seen these before!" cried Nip. "Some of the pilgrims have them."

"I've never seen one of these up close," said Billowtail. "May I hold it?" It was cool to the touch like a stone, but seemed to be made of thin bone.

"What are these?" asked Nip, taking it from Billowtail.

"Be careful," said Billowtail. "Don't drop it."

"I don't know what it is," said Ivy. "I've always wondered. When I hold it, I wish to know many things. To go to many distant places. To go, especially, where this came from."

"You wish to go to distant places?" asked Billowtail.

"Yes," said Ivy. "Very much so."

"I have never known a tree squirrel to wish for distant places," said Billowtail. "Mostly we just wish for close ones."

Ivy laughed shyly. "It must be in my blood. My ancestors were migrants."

"Migrants? Why?"

"There is only legend to tell the story as only a small number of us survived it. But for some reason, my grandparents felt they had to leave a place far away. Maybe there was no food. Or maybe there was disease. My mother was one of the few survivors, but she was not much more than a pinky, just old enough to eat solid food. She was taken in and given shelter by an elderly gray squirrel who had long since passed her pinky-bearing years."

"So, where did you get this?" asked Nip handing the object back to her.

"It was dropped by one of the Great Pinkies." She held it to her chest, wrapping both arms around it. "And I had the good fortune of finding it."

"Do you think it brings good fortune?" Billowtail asked.

"No," said Ivy. "But it brings thoughts of good fortune."

"We could sure use some of that right now," said Sugarcoat, gazing at the sky.

They all sat quietly for a few moments, thinking philosophical thoughts.

"Look up there," said Sugarcoat. "Do you know what the Great Pinkies call that swoosh of stars and fuzzy white glow around it?"

Billowtail, Nip and Ivy exchanged glances.

Billowtail shook his head. "What do they call it, Sugarcoat?"

"They call it El Camino Santiago."

"What does that mean?" asked Nip.

"No disrespect intended, Miss Sugarcoat," Ivy said with wrinkled forehead. "But how would you know? No squirrel can speak human."

"That is true," Sugarcoat said. "I don't speak it, but I once understood it, and I listened very closely to every word. And now it is as if I have a part of something bigger in me."

Ivy seemed to understand. Billowtail and Nip could not quite grasp it, but they found comfort in the fact that Ivy did, as the last thing they needed was something else from Sugarcoat's mouth that would add to the body of evidence that she was losing her mind.

"In most of the world, they call it the Milky Way," Sugarcoat continued. "But here, they call it El Camino Santiago, which means 'The Way of St. James.' This is the same name they give to the route to Compostela, the route we are following now, here on the ground."

"They have the same name for the route in the sky and the route on the earth?" Nip asked.

"Yes, exactly." Sugarcoat was pleased at his comprehension.

"I am glad Puttermunch isn't up there," Nip said, gazing at the stars. "I would hate to have to walk that."

"They call those stars El Camino Santiago because legend holds that it was formed from all the dust billowing up from the footsteps of pilgrims on the Way of St. James throughout the centuries," Sugarcoat said.

"You know what that means, don't you?" Ivy said, excitedly.

"What?" asked Billowtail.

"At least a few of those dust specks up there," she said dreamily, "are from your feet."

"Doesn't seem like my little feet could be of any consequence to the universe," said Billowtail.

"Every foot is of consequence to the universe," Ivy said.

"Do you know what Compostela means?" Sugarcoat continued her lesson.

They all shook their heads and looked intently into her face.

"It means 'field of stars.'"

"Field of stars," Ivy pondered as she gazed into the sky. "Field of stars."

"There is something beyond us," Sugarcoat said. "Do you see it?"

"I see stars," said Nip.

"And dust," added Billowtail.

"Me too," said Ivy. "But I feel something more."

"What?" asked Billowtail, moving closer to her and looking into her face. "What do you feel?"

"I do not have a word for it," Ivy said. "Sugarcoat, do the humans have a name for it?"

"I do not know."

"I doubt it," said Ivy. "I don't see how anybody could."

Billowtail watched Ivy watching the sky for a very long time. The thought did cross his mind that Sugarcoat was delusional and had made up the whole thing. But it seemed true, and he wanted to believe it.

"Why have you never told us this before, Sugarcoat?" Billowtail asked.

"It never seemed like the right time."

"Well, tonight is the perfect night," Billowtail said.

Ivy closed her eyes and took a deep breath through her nose, which was still trained upward into the night sky.

"The perfect night indeed," she smiled.

CHAPTER NINETEEN

MADE FOR GREATNESS

THE FOUR SQUIRRELS followed the Great Pinkies the whole of the following day. They crossed two rivers and one bridge, a ravine, a meadow and a woodland. Billowtail was impressed and surprised at Ivy's stamina, especially for someone who had never traveled.

As the sun set, Nip and Sugarcoat found several trees clustered near the Great Pinky camp, ran up the trunks and settled on some branches where they would rest for the night. At the base of one of the trees, Billowtail found a hole abandoned by a small animal and offered it to Ivy. She declined. Given that somebody had decided to move out, she said, it was probably infested with mites. But Billowtail insisted that he had checked every square inch of it and it turned up clean. He said he wouldn't take "no" for an answer and led her gently by the arm down several rungs of branches, escorting her to the opening of the habitat. He felt indebted to her for joining The Alliance, as if she were doing him a personal favor, even though when he stopped to think about it, this really made no sense. She surely had her own reasons for making the journey.

If Billowtail was going to be honest, there might have been something not quite so selfless in his turning over the nest to Ivy. He wasn't ready to go to bed yet. He wanted to talk to Sugarcoat about something. He found her awake in the next tree over, and after the initial startle at hearing his voice, she seemed glad to see him.

"Well, Billowtail," she said with a slight smile. "What are you doing awake? I would have thought you would have been bone-ache tired."

"I guess my bones do ache a bit. Quite a bit, actually. But I don't much notice it anymore. Unless I think about it."

"Well, then, we should have other things to think about."

"There is something, actually. That I have been thinking about. It's something you said."

"What's that?"

"That there is more to someone than bones."

"Yes, that is what the Great Pinkies believe."

"Back there in that place, the place I was hiding, I felt something."

"Something?"

"There was this piece of wood the Great Pinkies place their lips on, and later when everyone was gone, I got to touch it. And that's when I felt like there was someone there with me. Without bones. But still there."

"Must have been what the boy was talking about." A faraway look came over her. "I heard him having a discussion about it with some others."

"And something else too," Billowtail continued. "That soiled piece of cloth. The people, some of them had water draining from their eyes." Billowtail knew what that was about as a fair share had poured from his eyes during this journey. But his eye pouring was in response to losing something treasured and knowing it was his own folly that led to the loss. These human eyes were pouring at the sight of a piece of fabric.

"The cloth, the cloth, the cloth," Sugarcoat rubbed her head as she pondered. "Why would a cloth be so valuable to them?"

"And a soiled one at that."

Sugarcoat took a large amount of breath very quickly and looked at Billowtail with wide, understanding eyes. "Maybe it's not dirt. Maybe it's blood."

"What?"

"I heard the Great Pinkies speak of this occasionally. Maybe it's the blood that saved the world."

Billowtail sighed and looked down at his feet. His fears for Sugarcoat's mental health were returning. "But how could—"

"It seems it is custom among some of the Great Pinkies to place a cloth over the face of someone after they die, if the face has been disfigured. Maybe this is the cloth I heard them speak of long ago in our journey, the one that covered the disfigured face of the one who suffered to save the world."

"Save the world from what?"

"I'm not sure."

"Sugarcoat, are you feeling OK? I mean, are you feeling like yourself lately?"

"Not at all," she said. "I haven't felt like myself in many miles." She suddenly got very still and dropped her voice to something just above a whisper. "And yet, in some ways, I feel more like myself than I ever have in my whole life."

The contradictory and cryptic response did nothing to comfort Billowtail, but it seemed that if Sugarcoat had a disease, the illness would have shown some sort of physical affects by now.

"I have never experienced so much discomfort as I have since I joined The Alliance," Sugarcoat said. "But maybe we were not made for comfort. Maybe we were made for greatness."

Billowtail stretched out as long as he could go on the branch and watched the leaves dance between him and the endless field of stars, like points of light shining though pinholes pricked in black silk.

"We will need to get some sleep now, Billowtail," Sugarcoat said, yawning. "Our imaginations can carry us away when we're star gazing, but when the sun rises, it is our feet that will have to carry us. So we best rest while we can."

A thought struck Billowtail, and he wondered why he hadn't considered it before. Maybe the arrow that lodged in Sugarcoat had some kind of poison on it, a kind that would make you slowly lose your mind. The thought of it made him grieve yet again in his depths. Sugarcoat had talked more to him on that night than she had in the whole journey. Well, maybe not more, but deeper. She seemed now like a squirrel to him, not like another being of some sort. She seemed more ordinary, more vulnerable, more like him.

"Billowtail," Sugarcoat's voice interrupted his thoughts. "Are you asleep yet?"

"No. I don't think so."

"I think I will tell you something. I know I can trust you to keep my confidence."

This made Billowtail nervous. What if she told him something he needed to tell the others, for her sake or the sake of The Alliance or the mission? He didn't want to promise to keep any secrets.

"Now that Sir Sniff is gone," she said, not waiting for any protests, "someone else should have this information. I told him at the beginning of our journey and now that we are at what looks like the end, it is clear none of us knows who's going to make it and who is going to fall. So, in case something happens to me—"

"No, Sugarcoat, no. Nothing is going to happen to you."

Billowtail wondered if she knew her time was short. Maybe she had recognized the signs of her own sanity failing. How frightening it must be for her. "You're going to make it, Sugarcoat. We're all going to make it. Whatever it is you have to tell me, you can tell me at the end of our mission. You can tell me after we return Puttermunch safely home."

Billowtail realized how foolish he was. If Sugarcoat did indeed know her time was short, he should hear what she has to say. On the other hand, if she is losing her mind, what she has to say would be of little consequence, since it could be completely fabricated. Anyway, he couldn't bear the thought of losing another friend, and so, he refused to grant Sugarcoat permission to talk about the possibility.

"It's about the magic thread, Billowtail. About its origins."

"Sugarcoat," came an intense whisper from the bottom of the tree. "Are you up there?"

"Is that you, Nip?"

"Yes, it's me. I can't find Billowtail."

"He's here."

Nip scurried up the tree. "What are you two doing?"

"We were just talking," said Sugarcoat. "What are you doing up?"

"Couldn't sleep."

"Did you see Ivy?" asked Billowtail.

"Nope. I think she is still in the nest you found her," Nip said, looking over in that direction, with no hope of seeing that far in the dark.

"So, here we are," Billowtail said, "the ones who have travelled so many miles and should be exhausted enough to sleep. And the one who just joined the journey is sleeping soundly."

"She has not seen what we have seen," said Sugarcoat. "She does not have these things swirling in her head when she closes her eyes."

"What do you have swirling?" asked Billowtail.

Sugarcoat closed her eyes and dropped her head slightly.

"I have dead trees and badgers," said Nip. "Eagle's talons and arrows. Bulls and bridges."

"That's about what I have too," said Billowtail. "And you, Sugarcoat? What is keeping you awake?"

"At the moment, two very talkative young squirrels," said Sugarcoat. "Now, let's sleep."

Out of obedience or out of exhaustion, Billowtail and Nip complied almost immediately.

Nip was the first one to awaken the next morning, so he was the one to have to bear the bad news.

"Our Great Pinkies are gone! And so is Ivy."

The three had been up so late, that when sleep finally did take them, it took them deep. Sugarcoat, Nip and Billowtail did not hear the sunrise departure of the pilgrims, nor were they awakened by the early light of dawn filtering through their eyelids. By now, morning was fully underway, and the three went into a panic, discussing what to do now that they had been left behind.

"Do you think Ivy went with them?" asked Billowtail.

"I am sure she did," Sugarcoat said.

"Why would she leave without us?" Billowtail asked in something close to a panic. "Why didn't she wake us?"

"Maybe there wasn't time," Nip said. "Maybe she didn't know where we were, and she didn't have time to try to find us."

Sugarcoat offered an alternate theory: "Maybe she decided to go home when she awoke and found the Great Pinkies gone and us too."

Billowtail wasn't sure how he'd grown so attached to someone so quickly, but it was clear from how far his heart sunk at the thought of never seeing her again that something unusual had overtaken him.

"Well, let's not waste any time," said Sugarcoat, scurrying down the trunk with Billowtail and Nip on her heels. "We've got to try to catch up."

"Awww, I was so looking forward to breakfast," Nip called, already winded and panting. "The smell of pinecones was taunting me all night."

"Really, Nip, how can you think of food?" Billowtail admonished,

"If you weren't so lovesick, you'd be thinking about it too," said Nip.

"Lovesick? Why, I am not—" The two of them stopped at the base of the tree in preparation for a friendly quarrel.

"Boys, boys, we have no time for this," Sugarcoat said, taking them by the arms and pushing them along. "We have to go. Now."

CHAPTER TWENTY

A FIRE UNSEEN

LOOK," SAID NIP, STANDING in the middle
of the road, watching a dust blur approach.
"A trio of knights on horseback. I think we
should try to hitch a ride."

"No," said Sugarcoat. "It's far too dangerous."

Moving out of tree shade, into the sunlight, the
colors on the shields and horses' adornments grew
in vibrancy and made it all the more enticing for
Nip, whose eyes had grown fond, over the course
of the journey, to a kind of dazzle that is too much
for your typical country squirrel.

"But, we can each have our own horse," Nip
said, his gaze fixed. "It's perfect."

"What? No. Look," said Billowtail. "They're
speeding up. You can't possibly think we could—"

"Think how fast we would be able to go," said
Nip. "Come on!"

As the horses approached, enveloped in a field

of dust, Nip yelled, "Now!" and leapt into the brown cloud, catching a leather strap dangling off the saddle of the closest horse. Billowtail leapt too, but only after a second of delay as he tried to decide if it was wise or not. It was not. Billowtail caught the stirrup, but the forward momentum immediately detached his fingers from the iron, and he plummeted into the swoosh of earth the horses left behind.

"Oh, no!" he cried as he watched Nip recede into the distance. He heard a faint cry "Billowtail! Sugarcoat! I'll see you there." Then Billowtail looked behind him, and there stood Sugarcoat in the middle of the road, hands on her hips.

"I guess he didn't consider that these things take a bit of planning," Billowtail said, brushing the dust off his fur. He scrubbed his two front teeth with the back of his paw to get the sand off. "Let's go, Sugarcoat. We've got to catch up."

Sugarcoat shook her head as they began to walk. "There will be no catching up," she said. "The best we can hope for is a reunion when we all reach the destination. I just hope we can all find our way."

"As long as we're going in the direction opposite home, we are going the right way."

"I don't want to go home either, Billowtail. I have lost something precious as well. I am returning without the magic thread."

"No disrespect intended, Sugarcoat, but how could that be likened to Tippy's life?" Billowtail knew there was an edge to his voice, and he didn't like it—not when speaking to Sugarcoat. But it couldn't be helped. The value of a thing, magic or not, could not compare to that of a squirrel. "Anyway, the loss of the thread is my fault not yours. As is the loss of Tippy."

"No, the thread was my responsibility. I will not lay the blame on anyone else. If I had kept it safe, we would still have it today. I should not have taken it off."

"You only took it off because you thought we might be going into battle. I should never have taken advantage."

"Be that as it may, to return without it, there will be an unpayable debt. There is only one magic thread, and it can never be replaced, no matter how sorry I am or how many other things I am willing to give to make up for it."

"And so it is with me and my responsibility for the loss of Tippy," Billowtail said.

"We are agreed. But we can't run forever, Billowtail."

They walked a ways in silence, then jogged a bit, then returned to a fast walk.

Sugarcoat broke the silence. "You recall there was something I wanted to tell you back at La Hermosa. Now, that we are down to two, I feel it is imperative that someone else have this information."

"Down to two? No, we still have Nip. He's just not with us at the moment. And there's Ivy."

"Yes," Sugarcoat said. "As far as we know, we still have them. But please indulge me and hear my story."

"OK, Sugarcoat."

"You recall that I received the magic thread from the eldest ground squirrel at Bon Arbre. His name is Flickertail. He and his entire colony witnessed a most amazing event, not long ago, maybe three summers past. This is how he told it to me, the day we left to find Puttermunch:

There was once a church by a river, near the place where the ground squirrels lived before their migration to Bon Arbre. Inside the church was a man in robes of black and white. His name was Dominic. One day, some people from a place across the channel (they call them "the English") were on a pilgrimage to the tomb of St. James, and were crossing the river by the church. The boat capsized and the people were in danger of drowning. Dominic heard their cries and got down on his knees to do something the humans call *praying.*"

"I've seen that before!" Billowtail said. "At the places with the piece of wood and the soiled cloth. I have seen people do that! What does it mean? Why do they do it?"

"I don't know exactly. But in this case, it made the people who were drowning float to the top of the water and drift to shore where they were pulled from the water unharmed."

"Great Pinkies don't swim?" Billowtail asked.

"Many do not," Sugarcoat said. "According to Flickertail."

"Did Dominic?"

"I do not know."

"If he had, he would have jumped in and saved them, wouldn't he?"

"He could have only saved one, if he had jumped in. Praying saved all of them."

"Do all Great Pinkies do it?"

"What? Pray?"

"Yes."

"I do not know. It is so powerful, I assume that they do, since it would be quite foolish not to."

"Are they ever foolish like we are?"

"I do not know. Even with as much time as I have spent listening to them, I cannot answer that question. I do know they seem to need to be saved quite often. Seems to me that's why they are walking this road. To be saved from something." She had that faraway look like someone trying to remember something. "Well now, I do digress, do I not? We were talking about how the thread fell into the paws of the Swiftail Colony."

"Yes," said Billowtail. "Please do continue."

"Well, after all the pilgrims were taken care of by the people on the riverbanks and sent safely on their way, the squirrels were out collecting materials for their nest and they found this thread on a thorn bush near the church. Flickertail detangled it from among the briars and draped it around his neck, as it had tied itself into a sort of circle that was perfect for wearing. He intended to use it for the burrow he was lining. But a remarkable thing caught his attention as some people passed by on their way into the church. He could understand the words they spoke. They were speaking of this Dominic and how he had the gift of tongues."

"Tongues? He had multiple tongues?"

"Languages. Tongues are languages. What it means in their vocabulary is that he could understand and be understood by people who speak all kinds of different languages."

"Even Squirrelish?"

"No, no," Sugarcoat smiled. "Just the human languages."

"There is more than one?"

"Oh yes. Just as we and the field mice and the ground squirrels have different dialects and different words for the same item, so do the Great Pinkies."

"And the thread. It works on all the Great Pinky languages?"

"All that I know of."

"You still haven't told me where the thread came from."

"Yes, I told you it came from the thorn bush."

"But before that. Threads don't grow on bushes."

"Yes, that's true. Unless maybe they are cottonwood."

Billowtail smiled.

"Legend says the thread belonged to the robe of Dominic."

"Legend? I thought you said this happened just a few seasons ago. Aren't legends supposed to be old?"

"Either old now or old someday."

Billowtail didn't know what she meant by that. It was one of those many things she had said recently that made no sense, and he fought the temptation to doubt her entire story. It had to be true, didn't it? What else would explain the fact that they could understand the humans when they had possession of the thread?

"Anyway," Sugarcoat continued, "the Swiftails were able to glean quite a bit of information about Dominic by listening to the village folk recounting the story for passers through town. After that day of the great miracle, as they called it, there was substantial interest in knowing who this man was. There are all kinds of stories about how he chose the uncomfortable things, like being hungry when there was no shortage of food, eating two eggs, for instance, when there were more to be had. And avoiding the fire when his clothes were wet while the rest of his associates would huddle around the warmth. And yet his clothes would dry first, leading everyone to believe there is some other kind of fire that cannot be seen, and that's what dried his clothes."

"An invisible fire?"

"Yes, a fire unseen. That's what they said. And when he was still inside his mother's womb, she had a dream about a dog carrying a flaming torch in his mouth. And he was going to set the world on fire."

Billowtail gasped. "A dog with fire in its mouth?"

"But this dog was supposed to be good, and the fire is supposed to be good too."

Billowtail wished Sugarcoat would not say such ridiculous things. It made him lose all hope in the journey to think she was going insane. He had seen what pets could do and he had seen what fire could do.

"It was a pet that took Tippy from us, Sugar-coat. And it was a fire that took Sir Sniff."

"A fire?"

"If it wasn't for the forest fire, whoever dug those tunnels would still be living there. And we would have been in trees instead of tunnels and the badger could not have gotten us."

"You have grown in wisdom, Billowtail, since this journey began. But not all words are as they sound."

"Grown in wisdom," Billowtail scoffed. "Then, why do I know so little? So much less than I used to?"

"Wisdom requires you to know that you know little."

Sugarcoat and Billowtail picked up their speed again and ran awhile in silence. They came to a river and drank.

"There is also another story about him going around." Sugarcoat said. "Something I heard from the boy. Something that happened just this year."

"About who?"

"This man named Dominic."

"Oh, Dominic."

"Yes. A lady came from the sky and gave him a weapon."

"A weapon. What kind of weapon? "

"One for fighting lies."

"How do you fight lies?"

"According to the humans, you do it with a string of beads and some words, repeated and re-peated again, until your heart melts."

"Sounds dangerous."

"No, it's the kind of battle that can only bring you life."

"Sugarcoat, I mean this with all respect due to someone as obviously gifted in so many ways, but do you feel there is something wrong with your mind?"

"You mean have I lost it?"

"Y—yes. Have you lost it?

"Of course not. I know right where it is. Why do you ask, Billowtail?"

"There are times when the words you choose, the things you say, sometimes they just don't make much sense. With all due respect." He gave a little bow of the head.

Sugarcoat smiled and looked down at her paws, first the backs of them, then the front, then the backs again. "How do you know?" she asked kindly.

Billowtail didn't know how to answer that. So many examples flooded his head, but he wouldn't have known how to convince anyone of the un-soundness of any given statement, other than to say it just sounded crazy.

"I have learned something from the Great Pin-kies," Sugarcoat said. "They spend their entire lives trying to figure things out, and that which they don't understand they study all the harder. But if even the Great Pinkies struggle to under-stand, we can't be surprised when a squirrel finds it hard to comprehend what an elder squirrel has learned from men."

"I wish we still had Dominic's thread. I'm so sorry, Sugarcoat."

"The losses here have been profound. But you have already been forgiven."

"We've lost the oldest and youngest member of The Alliance and the thread that was our only hope for completing the mission."

"Not our only hope."

"What other one do we have?"

"Hope is its own species. You can have it with-out having any other."

"See? That's what I'm talking about, Sugar-coat. Do you hear yourself?

"I do. I hear myself more clearly than I have ever heard myself before. Now let's run."

CHAPTER TWENTY-ONE

THE SECRET STONE

BILLOWTAIL AND SUGARCOAT ran and ran, surprised and pleased at their own stamina. They were able to ignore the rumbling in their bellies and the pinching feeling in their feet and the burning in their thighs, and they just ran, in hopes of finding another pilgrim, or even better, another member of The Alliance. What they found first was a place. There was something different about this one. It was alive with crowds of Great Pinkies, smiling and laughing, tired, but peaceful, speaking warmly to one another. They were watching, no, more like absorbing, the colorful parade that passed by—knights on horses, jugglers and musicians. Billowtail noticed that the colors no longer hurt his eyes, as they did at the beginning of the journey. He actually enjoyed them now. So, he watched intently, attending to every detail, and that's how he noticed something quite unexpected.

There behind the shield, just behind the saddle of one of the knights was a small set of ears, barely visible.

"Ivy!" Billowtail hollered. "Ivy, is that you?"

The head popped up over the shield, and up stretched a squirrel. She began waving frantically as she realized the parade was about to turn into a reunion.

"Billowtail! Billowtail!"

The knight turned at hearing the squeaking, and caught a glimpse of two squirrels leaping from his horse, into the crowd, causing a parting of the Great Pinkies, none of whom were keen on the possibility of a squirrel running up a leg, though why that came to mind is not exactly clear since squirrels rarely do this.

"What took you so long?" Nip asked, bounding toward Billowtail and playfully slapping him on the back. "You've got to get yourself some horsepower."

"We were travelling the old fashioned way," Billowtail said. "By squirrel power."

"It's not as fast, but just as sure," said Sugarcoat. "How long have you been here?"

"A while," said Nip, who was never the best at keeping track of time.

"And when did you get here, Ivy?" Billowtail asked.

"We arrived together," she replied. "Nip saw me walking on the side of the road, following the three Great Pinkies, and he picked me up on his galloping steed. He was hanging from the tail and grabbed me, and we climbed up the tail and perched on the rump and had a nice view of the road, actually. It was a surprisingly smooth ride considering we had nothing to hold onto."

"Nothing but some half-inch horse fur," said Nip, gloating.

"And I don't think the horse noticed a thing," Ivy added. "Oh, it was such fun!"

"But we've been working since we arrived here," Nip said, trying to restore some sobriety to the moment.

"Working?" Sugarcoat raised an eyebrow.

"Trying to find Puttermunch. Ivy took it upon herself to ask around and see if any of the locals had seen him. And oh, by the way, I think we are in Compostela."

Gifted with an honest face and a conversational style, Ivy was able to garner quite a bit of useful information from a number of sources.

"Apparently, the boy has tried releasing Puttermunch a number of times, and he won't go," Ivy said. "That's according to the local squirrels."

"The boy wants to be rid of him?" Billowtail asked.

"The boy wants him to have his freedom," Sugarcoat said.

"Why would Puttermunch not want that?" asked Nip.

"Puttermunch has never lived on his own," Sugarcoat said.

"There is another possibility," said Ivy.

"What?" Nip and Billowtail answered in unison.

"The squirrels were saying Puttermunch did not respond to them when they tried to say a few words to him. They surmised he either doesn't understand Squirrelish, doesn't care what they say, or he is deaf."

"Deaf?" Nip exclaimed.

"Or maybe he is just shy," said Billowtail.

"Or savvy enough not to talk to strangers," said Sugarcoat.

"So, how do we find the boy and his squirrel?" asked Nip. "We've been here for two days now, and there's no sign of them. It seems an impossibility now."

"Impossibility? Maybe in most places, but maybe not here," Sugarcoat said, a bit dreamily. "Let me see now, I hope I can get the story straight." She closed her eyes and rubbed her forehead vigorously and then opened her eyes again. They were clear and fixed on something distant. "There was once a type of Great Pinky they call a hermit."

"Yes, I have heard of them," said Ivy. "They live in the sea. They are crabs."

"No, this one lived on land. A hermit is a variety of Great Pinky who lives by himself."

"Kind of like a squirrel," Nip said.

"Yes," Sugarcoat said, "but for different reasons, which I do not understand, so do not ask, as I was not able to glean that from any conversation."

"Well, why do squirrels do it?" Nip asked.

"We were made that way," said Sugarcoat.

"But not hermits?" asked Nip.

"They do it because they choose to," Sugarcoat said. "It's different for them. Anyway, this particular hermit saw flashes of light coming from the forest. He reported it to another type of Great Pinky called a bishop, which I guess is something like a king."

The word "king" struck sadness in Billowtail's heart as he remembered how his king had died for him.

"An investigation led to the discovery of a tomb, and a church was built in honor of the man who was buried there. They call him St. James and he was a very good friend of a great king. And that has been the reason for this trek all the Great Pinkies make past our tree in Bon Arbre, over mountains, across the plains, along shores and through forests."

"All of that to visit someone who is dead?" Ivy asked.

"Well, technically," Sugarcoat said, "St. James is not dead, according to the Great Pinky way of thinking."

"Not dead?" Billowtail asked, "Didn't you say they found him buried there in the flashing forest?"

"Yes, but those are just his bones. The other part of him is alive."

"The other part?" Ivy asked.

"The part you cannot see."

The squirrels decided to look for the boy in the place where the chances of finding a Great Pinky is greatest—namely, where there is a crowd of Great Pinkies. They would have rather retreated to the nearby woods for a celebratory meal. A celebration would have been in order, since they were all reunited again. Plus, they could have used an excuse to eat. They had burned a great many calories. But it was a good thing they had decided to ignore their stomachs because almost immediately upon entering the center of the village, they saw the boy's horse, Gimblerigg, tied to a stake.

"No, kid, no!" came a voice from a single tree next to a row of shops. "Don't go down that way. It's a trap!"

Billowtail looked up into the tree and saw an elderly squirrel holding the tail of a baby squirrel, keeping him from sliding down a pole that was propped at a slant against the tree. "That's a squirrel pole, son," the old squirrel explained, to the wide-eyed young one. "Humans know squirrels are lazy and would rather climb down a slanted pole than a straight-up-and-down tree. Takes less energy, you know. So they set that pole there, with a snare at the bottom, and bam!" He smacked one hand against the other. "One more squirrel in the stew pot."

The baby squirrel got loose and ran straight down the tree trunk, and looking back at the squirrel pole, slammed right into Sugarcoat.

"Puttermunch!" Billowtail exclaimed.

"Puttermunch," said Sugarcoat, holding the squirrel gently by the upper arms and looking into his face. "We've come to take you home."

"Home?" The young squirrel looked disturbed by that word.

"Yes, we've come on a long journey to find you and bring you back to the place you were born," Sugarcoat said. "You fell from the nest in a place called Bon Arbre. There are many squirrels back there waiting for you to come home and one in particular."

"But my boy, he take good care of me. He no like squirrels. But he like me. He save me from dog last day. And he tell me I cute and feed me nuts and sometimes bread. Oh, yummy bread! And he take me places. So many places! But maybe not so many anymore. He like stay here. There lots of horses to put shoes on here."

"But the boy wants you to go free," Billowtail said. "And live the life of a squirrel."

"And be happy," said Nip.

"And your mother, Mrs. Poggins, she has been crying, you can bet, ever since you fell," said Billowtail.

"And oh, by the way, you are a Poggins," said Sugarcoat. "You are Puttermunch Poggins of Bon Arbre."

"Wait a minute," Billowtail said. "Did you say he calls you cute?"

"Yeah, my boy call me 'cute' and 'rascal.'"

"You can understand him?" Sugarcoat asked.

"Only when I wearing the string."

"The magic thread? You have the magic thread?" Sugarcoat's eyes glistened. "Oh, Puttermunch, I cannot tell you how relieved I am. You are safe. The magic thread is found. What a glorious day!" She closed her eyes and pointed her nose into the sky.

"Magic?" Now Puttermunch's eyes lit up.

"Well, that's what we call it," said Sugarcoat. "But I think we have discovered that it must be so much more than that. Where is it? Do you have it?"

"My squirrel friend tell me to hide it. Keep it safe, so it not get lost."

"I am puzzled about something," said Ivy. "If you were raised by cats, how can you speak Squirrelish?"

"When I little, I not know why I not able to speak cattish. So I don't speak nothing to nobody. Then I meet squirrels and they make these strange noises and I try it and I can make them too, and I good at it. Then this nice squirrel teach me. He say one day I need to talk Squirrelish. Maybe I go live with squirrels one day. In a place with lots of shade and nuts and a stream of fresh water. That the story he tell me."

"That's exactly it, Puttermunch," said Billowtail. "That's exactly why we came. To take you to the place that squirrel spoke of to you."

"I like him stories. He make up good ones. But I stay with my boy. He give me food and shade."

"Can you take us to the magic thread now, Puttermunch?" asked Sugarcoat.

"Now? But I waiting for my boy. Him, uh, *he* buying stuff. Maybe he get me some bread!"

"And where do you keep the thread?" Sugarcoat said. "In a safe place, I hope."

"Uh-huh. Under a secret stone."

"Where? Where is this secret stone? You will

be able to show us, right?"

"I dunno" Puttermunch said thoughtfully. "It a secret."

A look of near-panic overtook Sugarcoat's face.

"But I show you," Puttermunch said with a buoyant smile. "If I remember where."

Sugarcoat closed her eyes and wrinkled her forehead. Billowtail knew what she was thinking. What are the chances of a young squirrel being able to return to a magic thread, small and scentless, and hidden under one of a billion rocks in this great big world?

CHAPTER TWENTY-TWO

THE TUTOR

"JUST A LITTLE BIT MORE FAR," said Puttermunch, skipping and watching his tail behind him, as young squirrels often do when their tails are newly fluffed and, to their own selves, captivatingly lovely. The tiny squirrel had four larger ones following him in wavy lines. Wavy because, though Puttermunch could have gone from point A to point B in a straight line on flat ground, he insisted on straying up over rocks, down into hollows, through thickets and around tree trunks in spirals. He obviously did not feel the same sense of urgency that the other squirrels felt. They had convinced him that it would be alright to leave his boy behind long enough to take The Alliance where they needed to go.

"Right there," said Puttermunch, pointing deeper into the forest. "Right into those trees and out of the trees and then stop at big rock by stream. Well, I go now." He was fixing to go scampering off in wavy lines back the way they came.

"Wait, Puttermunch, wait! Where are you going?"

"I have to go back to my boy. He can no find me if I here."

"No, no," said Sugarcoat. "You have to stay with us. We can't lose you again."

"Oh I no be lost. I be with my boy."

"But Puttermunch, we came to bring you home."

"Who goes there?" A voice from above came bellowing from the tree. Nip and Billowtail looked at each other with round eyes, read each other's thoughts and then turned their eyes up the tree. A small head popped out from the leaves. Nip grabbed Billowtail's arm and squeezed tight enough for his claws to poke past the fur and make indentations in his flesh. Billowtail did not feel a thing.

"Tippy!" Sugarcoat shouted, running up the tree.

"Sugarcoat!" The agile red squirrel ran down to meet her and threw his arms around her. "You're finally here!"

They both flew down the tree, their feet scarcely touching the bark.

"Tippy! Tippy! Tippy!" Billowtail, Nip and Tippy slammed themselves into one massive huddle, laughing uncontrollably. A droplet formed on the outer corner of each of their eyes. Billowtail wanted to enter a full-blown cry, but he didn't want to get everyone's fur soaked. Sugarcoat placed one hand on Billowtail's shoulder and the other on Tippy's, adding a second layer to the embrace. Ivy looked on with a large smile.

"Tippy, how on earth?" Billowtail exclaimed.

"How in the world?" cried Nip.

"How is it possibly you?"

"How can it be?"

"Oh, yeah, this my Squirrelish teacher," Puttermunch said running straight into the middle of the hug, displacing Nip and Billowtail and throwing Tippy off balance.

"Ha, Puttermunch," Tippy said, steadying himself and then tweaking the young squirrel's ear. "You done good bringing my friends back to me." His large smile, his high eyebrows and the rest of his face froze in place as he looked around, over the heads of the jubilant squirrels. "Where's Sir Sniff?"

Billowtail, Sugarcoat and Nip exchanged glances, waiting for the other to say what was so devastating to say.

"I'm afraid," said Ivy stepping up, "your valiant Sir Sniff did not make it. He gave his life for the others."

"No." The joy on Tippy's face crashed into bewilderment. "How?"

"He saved us from a badger," said Sugarcoat. "I am very sorry Tippy. We are all grief stricken as I know you are."

"Yes," said Tippy softly, lowering himself slowly to a sitting position and propping his back against the tree trunk.

The rest of the squirrels sat down around him, first Nip, then Billowtail, then Sugarcoat and Ivy.

"Can we go now?" asked Puttermunch, rolling a roundish pinecone around in circles in a small clearing nearby.

"Just a minute, Puttermunch," Sugarcoat said. "We'll leave shortly."

"But, my boy," he complained. "He not know where I am. I want to go now."

"He *will* not know where I am," Tippy corrected, giving the rest of the squirrels hope that he would recover from the loss of Sir Sniff.

"Tippy," said Billowtail gently. "We're eager to

know. How did you survive? We all thought you were—" Billowtail didn't want to say it. He had lived it too vividly already.

"The eagle saved me. He flew me to this place. Oh, it's such an amazing thing to fly. The speed, it's so exhilarating, and being lost in the sky. Even being close to death, I felt more alive than ever."

"The flight made you well?" Billowtail asked.

"No, it was not the flight. It was this place. The place made me well."

"Compostela," Sugarcoat said.

"The man in the brown robe," said Billowtail, a look of peace returning to his face. "He saved you. You were going to die of a cat bite. Only an eagle could have carried you swiftly enough. So he called his friend from the sky to come and get you and take you to a place where you could be made well."

"Was there a doctor?" Sugarcoat asked.

"No, just a large shiny place where many people were coming to find something or to be healed."

"Yes," Sugarcoat said. "A church. The Church of St. James. I heard people call it Santiago de Compostela."

"Yes!" Tippy said. "That's it! I have heard that word many times. Santiago!"

"Tell us how it happened, Tippy," said Ivy in her smooth, enthusiastic voice. "Tell us how you were healed."

"Uh, sure," said Tippy. "But first, do you mind if I ask who you are? I mean, you're very nice and everything—"

"I'm sorry," said Billowtail. "I never introduced you. This is Ivy Silkpocket. She joined The Alliance to help us find Puttermunch."

"I not lost," said Puttermunch, somersaulting along a log. "But I want my boy."

"I *am not* lost," corrected Tippy.

Billowtail never knew Tippy to be such a stickler for grammar, but maybe the journey and the brush with death had matured him.

"So Tippy," said Billowtail, "what exactly did happen?"

"The eagle flew me right through the open door of this gigantic building."

"The Cathedral," Sugarcoat said.

"And, passing over the heads of all the Great Pinkies—their eyes were all wide and their mouths gaping open and they had to duck to avoid the whoosh of the eagle's wings—that mighty bird flew me right above this grand table and placed me in the lap of a wooden man seated there, like on a throne, as if watching all that happens down below."

"The likeness of St. James," Sugarcoat said.

"I was only there for what seemed like maybe just three flaps of the eagle's wings," Tippy continued, "and then he swooshed me away, back out of the—what did you call it, Sugarcoat?"

"The Cathedral?" Ivy answered.

"Yes, the Cathedral," said Tippy.

"And then you were OK?" Nip asked, excitedly.

"Oh no," Tippy said in earnest. "I was more than OK. I was the best I had ever been in my life."

"So the wood healed you," Billowtail summarized, remembering the wood in that place earlier in the journey. The one the Great Pinkies pressed their lips to. "That makes sense, I guess."

"No, Billowtail," Sugarcoat said. "It is not the wood. It is what the wood represents."

"The man then," said Billowtail. "St. James."

"No, as far as I can tell, not the man either," Sugarcoat said. "But the one the man is friends with."

"Wait a minute! Wait a minute!" Nip cried with urgency not common for Nip. "Where's Puttermunch?"

"Oh no!" said Billowtail, looking around frantically. "Don't tell me he slipped away from us."

They canvassed the area calling his name.

"How could we have let this happen?" said Sugarcoat. "What fools we are!"

"Well he won't be hard to find," said Ivy. "We know where he's headed."

"The thread," Sugarcoat said. "Puttermunch said it was here. Do you know where it is, Tippy?"

"Of course," he said rather smugly, though no one could have read smugness into any of Tippy's intentions. "It's under one of those rocks by the stream there."

Sugarcoat stared with wide eyes at the multitude of rocks banking the small trickle of water.

"One of them?" Sugarcoat said. "Which one?"

"Let me think," said Tippy, laying his finger crossways over his lips.

"There's not time," said Billowtail. "We've got to go after Puttermunch. Every minute counts. What if he finds the boy and they leave Compostela and we never find them again?"

"But we're so close to the thread," said Sugarcoat. "And understanding the Great Pinkies might be imperative to finding Puttermunch again."

"No," said Billowtail. "We've got to go."

"I'll stay here and try to remember where I put the thread," said Tippy. "You all go, and I'll meet you."

"Where?" asked Billowtail, putting his hands on Tippy's shoulders. "We don't want to lose you again either. Where will we meet and when?"

"Sunset at the Cathedral," Tippy said turning over rocks.

"I'll stay with Tippy and help look," said Ivy, pushing on a large stone.

"Good idea," said Billowtail. Actually, he thought it a crummy idea. He didn't want to be separated from Ivy. But it was the best possibility for finding both the thread and Puttermunch.

CHAPTER TWENTY-THREE

THE SQUIRREL CHAIN

BILLOWTAIL, NIP AND SUGARCOAT retraced their steps back to the village shop where Puttermunch's boy had been shopping. They found Puttermunch there in the same area where they had found him the first time. He was lying on his belly, stretched out flat, feet extended, arms straight out, and he might have looked dead if it was not for the fact that he was passing an acorn mindlessly from one hand to the other and back again.

"He gone," Puttermunch said, not looking up from his acorn.

"How do you know?" asked Billowtail. "Maybe he's still in the shop."

"Or in another shop," said Nip.

"No. The cart is gone," Puttermunch said with puddling eyes. It was the only home Puttermunch had ever known—the place he grew up under the warm protective care of the mother cat in the company of the playful litter that spent every waking moment together—and the sleeping ones too. Tippy had told Puttermunch that squirrels live in trees, and in time, he would grow accustomed to it. But Puttermunch didn't want to get used to it, even if it would have been possible. Of course, the cart was not the same since the cat and kittens were sold. It was actually quite empty and lonely. But at least it was a familiar place. And it was attached to the boy, who was never anything but good to him.

"Come home with us, Puttermunch," said Nip. "We'll show you the best of how squirrels should live. Your mother has been waiting and waiting for you to come home."

"I guess a mother might be nice to have," Puttermunch said, pushing himself into a sitting position.

"Yes," said Billowtail. "You should never take one of those for granted."

Sugarcoat laid a paw on Billowtail's shoulder, and he looked deep into her knowing eyes.

"Come on, Puttermunch," said Billowtail. "It's almost sunset and we've got to meet Tippy and Ivy at the Cathedral."

Puttermunch led the way. Although he was no expert on Compostela, he had been there considerably longer than the others and so had a much better idea of where things were. He didn't tell them that he was holding out hope of finding the boy there. The boy had gone frequently, passing through those large doors, sometimes sad, sometimes tired, sometimes hardened, and each time he had come out softer.

After a long wait, it became clear the boy wasn't going to come. And neither were Tippy and Ivy.

"We'll have to go back into the forest and look for them," said Billowtail.

"But it's dark now," said Nip. "How will we find

them? And what if they're just running late and they show up here, and we've already gone?"

"You stay here, Nip, and watch Puttermunch," said Sugarcoat. "It's far too dangerous to take him into the dark forest, not knowing what has delayed Tippy and Ivy."

"OK," said Nip.

Billowtail thought Nip was very quick to agree to this arrangement. He remembered his lack of valor back at the grapevines, and couldn't help but think Nip would not be a good one to have with you in times of great distress and need. For example, while walking into a deep dark forest to find missing friends. On the other hand, Sir Sniff had also failed Sugarcoat in the vineyard, and a number of sunsets later, he gave his life in the burnt forest.

Billowtail was comforted to be going with Sugarcoat, since she was probably the smartest of The Alliance and quite possibly the bravest. She was definitely the most level-headed. He had rarely seen her express emotion, and when she did it was never a breakdown, but rather very restrained. Billowtail just hoped Nip would be able to handle anything that came his way while Puttermunch was in his care.

At any rate, he was certain Puttermunch was safer where he was than in the dark forest, headed toward whatever it was that had delayed Tippy and Ivy.

Indeed, the forest launched Billowtail's imagination into a wild run, and his fear would have surely gotten the better of him if he wasn't so determined to find Tippy and Ivy.

Even Sugarcoat, with her uncanny ability to put aside her feelings in favor of logic, seemed to be feeling anxious thinking of all the dangerous things that lie in the dark.

"Wait, shhhh, listen!" Sugarcoat stopped cold in her tracks. "Is that—do you hear that?"

Billowtail froze, and cocked his head to listen. "It's Tippy! Coming from that direction." He pointed into the darkness to the west, which could not be distinguished from the darkness in the north, south or east. Billowtail took off running, with Sugarcoat at his heels, cautioning him to slow down lest he fall prey to a snarl of thickets, waiting to trip and disable him and render him an easy target for the talons of an owl or the jowls of some other nocturnal beast.

"Tippy! We're coming, buddy! Just keep talking. We're coming."

"Be careful," Tippy yelled. "There's a huge hole. I'm caught down in it."

It was unlike any hole any squirrel had ever seen before. It was deep and narrow and the sides were slick and solid and wet, and there was standing water at the bottom, hip-high to a squirrel.

"Tippy, are you OK?" Billowtail hollered into the hole.

"I want out," Tippy sounded close to panicked. "Can you get me out, Billowtail? Please?"

Billowtail looked at Sugarcoat.

"Of course we'll get you out," said Sugarcoat.

"Where's Ivy?" Billowtail asked.

"She's not with you?" asked Tippy. "She went to find help."

"No, we have not seen her," said Sugarcoat.

Tippy was bouncing up and down on his toes, making the water slosh around him. "It's cold, and I can't stand the wet for much longer. Can you get me out? Is there a way?"

"I assume you already tried climbing the walls."

"Too slippery. There's absolutely no foothold and nothing to sink my claws into."

"Maybe we can find a vine," Sugarcoat said, surveying the lush woods.

"Ivy looked everywhere," Tippy called up.

"Wait, shhh." Sugarcoat said. "Something is

coming."

"Two somethings," said Billowtail.

"Actually, three. Two regular-sized somethings and a smaller something."

Whatever they were, they were approaching at a fast pace. Billowtail and Sugarcoat scurried up a tree and held perfectly still, listening. Neither one liked the idea of having Tippy stuck in the well down below, but at least he was hidden from ground level. Still, what if whatever they were that were approaching fell into the hole with Tippy and devoured him? Or what if they were accomplished tree climbers and decided to come after Billowtail and Sugarcoat? As their footsteps got closer, it was clear they were travelling with purpose, maybe running from something or running toward something, perhaps to arrive at a place with ample prey and satisfy some ravenous hunger.

"It's around here somewhere," came a voice. It took a second for it to register, but Billowtail realized it was Ivy. "Tippy! Where are you?"

Billowtail and Sugarcoat breathed a sigh of relief and ran down the tree.

"Over here!" cried Tippy.

"Ivy! Over here!" echoed Billowtail.

"Billowtail!" came another voice.

"Nip!" cried Sugarcoat. "Where's Puttermunch?"

"Got him right here!" Nip yelled.

All the squirrels ran at top speed toward the sound of each other's voices, and collided into a flurry of fur, rolling along as one big unit, stopping short of the hole where poor Tippy craned his neck, looking up in a hopeless attempt to see what was happening in the darkness outside the dark, deep hole.

"I thought you were going to stay and keep Puttermunch safe," Sugarcoat said, standing up and brushing herself off.

"I was going to," said Nip, "but Ivy and I discussed it and decided maybe my help would be needed here. Don't worry. We have been and will continue to be vigilant in keeping Puttermunch safe."

"I safe," Puttermunch panted. "This is fun!"

"This is not a good place for a little one," Sugarcoat groused.

"I not little," the tyke said, standing on his tip toes.

"It would have perhaps been better," Sugarcoat said, "for you to have listened to the one who has been with you on this journey from the beginning, Nip. Not the late-comer."

Sugarcoat did not like the fact that she didn't like Ivy. She knew she was prejudging her, or even worse, that she was jealous of her. Sugarcoat has never been what any squirrel has ever considered attractive. The lack of color to her fur gave squirrels fodder for ridicule in her youth and reason to ignore her in her womanhood. There was not one other squirrel in Bon Arbre that looked anything like her. As she matured, it became less and less hurtful to be considered strange or invisible. Her lack of companionship caused her to become introspective, or what some would consider deep. For a squirrel, anyway. Squirrels are not usually concerned with much more than eating and occasionally playing and staying warm and unbitten by fleas, and, if you are a female, seeing your children to the age of tail fluff.

"Ideas, Sugarcoat?" Billowtail asked. "How are we going to get Tippy out of there?"

"Let's make he some wings," Puttermunch suggested.

"*Him*, Puttermunch!" Tippy called up. "Let's make *him* some wings."

"Let's go vine hunting," Nip suggested.

"In the dark?"

A wolf's howl rang out in the not-far-enough distance.

"We've got to get him out fast," Ivy said. "We are all just prey here, waiting to be eaten."

"Well," Billowtail said, "if there are no vines to throw down to Tippy, how about we make one?"

"Out of what?" asked Nip.

"Us," said Ivy, smiling at Billowtail, happy to be reading his mind. "We'll make one out of us. Oh, Billowtail, you are brilliant!"

"I am?"

"Yes," said Sugarcoat. "That is brilliant, Billowtail. OK, first we must determine who is the strongest. He will be the one at the top. He will have to support the weight of all the others."

"Or she," said Ivy.

"Or she," Sugarcoat agreed.

"Well, Billowtail is the largest," said Nip.

"Yes, but that does not mean he is the strongest," said Sugarcoat. "We must test everyone's strength. There, see that rock? Let us see which one of us can lift it."

They all tried in turn and each was able to lift it.

"We must find a larger rock," Sugarcoat said.

Billowtail set about rolling various sizes of rocks into a row, smallest to largest.

"Brilliant again, Billowtail!" Ivy exclaimed. "We will all lift larger and larger rocks until a winner is found,"

Indeed, it was Billowtail who could lift the largest rock, which surprised no one but himself. He exceeded them all in size, but he had never considered himself muscular, although he wouldn't know under all that fur. Next came Nip, then Sugarcoat, then Ivy, who was delicate-boned and had trouble lifting even the smallest rock. "Well, this is embarrassing," she said, grunting as she struggled to hoist it to chest height.

Billowtail took hold of the root of a tree stump adjacent to the well and held tight to it as he let his feet dangle into the mouth of the hole. Nip climbed down over him and grabbed onto his feet. Sugarcoat climbed over Billowtail and Nip and held onto Nip's feet. And finally Ivy climbed down over Billowtail, Nip, and Sugarcoat and held onto Sugarcoat's feet, becoming the final link in a perfect squirrel chain.

Perfect, but short. Almost three full squirrels too short.

"It's no use," Tippy said, stretching his arms as far as he could. "Not even close."

"Wait a minute!" cried Sugarcoat. "We are not making use of our most prized possessions!"

"Our tails!" Billowtail said. "Our tails!"

"Our tails?" Nip asked.

"If we add our tails to the chain," Sugarcoat said, "the chain will be that much longer." She was happy to be contributing the most to the effort, as she had an unusually long tail, and she was never more grateful for it than in this moment.

Billowtail grimaced at the thought of his tail having to support the weight of four squirrels. Not to mention, his hands were already feeling like giving out, even without Tippy's weight added to the "vine."

"OK, Billowtail," Sugarcoat said. "Let down your tail. Nip, grab on."

Billowtail's tail came fluffing into Nip's face, sending dust and flecks of forest soil into his nose and eyes. It had been quite some time since Billowtail had time to groom his tail. Nip wrinkled his nose and scrunched his eyes.

"Hurry, Nip," Billowtail said. "What are you waiting for?"

"I have to—I have to—ahhh—ahhhh—"

"No, Nip!" cried Billowtail. "No! Don't sneeze!"

"Hold it in, Nip," Sugarcoat demanded.

"Come on, Nip," Ivy coaxed. "You can do it. Just grab on."

Nip transferred his right hand from Billowtail's foot to his tail, sinking deep into the fur to find a good grip on the bone. Then he followed with his left. He worked his way down the tail as Billowtail continued to grimace.

"Please hurry everyone," he pleaded. "Please hurry."

Nip let down his tail and Sugarcoat grabbed on and then let hers down for Ivy.

Nip's sneeze threatened to return: "Ahhh—ahhhh—"

"No, Nip," Sugarcoat commanded. "You mustn't!"

Nip wrinkled his face and stifled his sneeze while Tippy reached for Ivy's tail. But the chain was still half of a squirrel too short and nothing Tippy could do, no amount of stretching or grunting or standing on tiptoe or jumping and attempting to grab was going to render the chain long enough. Billowtail grunted and squeezed his eyes together. "Hurry up down there," he pushed his words out through puffed cheeks, as if making his cheeks larger would add to his brawn.

"It's no use," Tippy cried. "I can't reach."

"If only we had one more squirrel," Nip said, still sniffing his sneeze in.

"Me!" cried Puttermunch from the top of the hole. "Me am another squirrel!"

"No!," yelled Tippy. "We are not risking your life. You are the reason we have come this far. We have to return you safely."

As is often the case with young squirrels, Puttermunch either did not hear or pretended not to, as he had already started down the squirrel chain before Tippy could finish his protest.

"No, Puttermunch," Billowtail said. "Go back."

"No, Puttermunch!" Nip echoed, as he felt the

young squirrel's claws moving quickly down his back. "Ahhh—ahhh—"

"No, Nip," Sugarcoat hollered, "no sneezing!"

Puttermunch's foot squished the skin on the top of her head down onto her forehead, wrinkling her eyes closed behind an accordion of skin. "Turn around right this instant, Puttermunch, and get out of this hole." Sugarcoat spoke in the most stern voice she had yet to muster in the entire span of her life. "You're going to fall in, and then we'll have twice the trouble."

"I not fall," Puttermunch said, perkily moving on past her back to her never-ending tail. "I never fall."

The irony of this statement made every squirrel in that squirrel chain roll his eyes. "Your falling is why we are here in the first place!" Tippy exclaimed. "Now get back up there."

Puttermunch had reached Ivy's tail and was hanging on with the grip of a thousand squirrels, despite his small hands.

"I ready, Tippy," he said. "Grab me tail."

"*My* tail," said Tippy. "And no, I will not."

"Why not?"

"I could pull you off and then you'll be stuck down here too."

"I not let go. Promise."

"Hurry," cried Billowtail, breathless. "I can't hold on much longer."

"Me neither," said Nip.

"Grab me tail," said Puttermunch. "I not leaving if you not grab me tail."

"What should I do, Sugarcoat?" Tippy yelled up.

Sugarcoat let out a sound somewhere between a grunt and a sigh. "OK, Tippy. Grab on."

"Yay!" Puttermunch exclaimed. "I gonna be a hero."

"Believe me, kid, you do not want to make that

your primary focus," said Billowtail.

Before any more could be said, Tippy had made his way up past Puttermunch, onto Ivy's back and made his way up the rest of the squirrel chain.

"Freedom!" he screamed when he got to the top, and out into the open air. "OK, Puttermunch, climb on up. It's a cinch."

Puttermunch scurried up the chain and had just made his way out of the hole when Tippy cried, "Owl! There are owl eyes in that tree, and they're looking right at us. Everybody stay where you are!" He threw his body over Puttermunch.

"Owl?!!" cried Billowtail. "Ughhh. I can't hold on any longer."

"Should we all just drop?" Nip asked.

"No!" cried Ivy, grabbing onto the fur above her and hoisting herself up over Sugarcoat, over Nip and over Billowtail to the top of the well, where she threw her body over Tippy's.

Sugarcoat followed in the same fashion, landing on top of Ivy. Then Nip on top of her and finally, Billowtail laid himself on top the entire squirrel pile. *If anyone is going to be eaten by an owl, it is going to be me.* The thought was terrifying, and he wondered what it would have felt like to be a brave squirrel. He wished he was not shaking from head to toe from the terror of the thought. He wished he could hold back the tears that were seeping from the outside corners of his eyes. He wished he could be glad to die for his friends, but he wanted desperately to hold on to his life. More desperately, though, he wanted each of them to live. So he held his position. And within seconds, the unthinkable that he had been thinking did indeed come to pass, and the owl swooped in on him and pierced his flesh, tugging and ripping at the loose skin of his back. It was, no doubt, perplexing for the owl, who had never had trouble carrying off a squirrel before. But this one was inordinately heavy, like it was made of iron, since Billowtail was holding so tightly to Nip, and Nip holding so tightly to Ivy and Ivy so tightly to Sugarcoat and Sugarcoat so tightly to Tippy, and Tippy (poor Tippy) was doing his best to make himself into an arch over Puttermunch so the tiny squirrel would not be crushed under the weight. And there was so much weight, that the owl struggled fiercely, and only after an intense amount of effort was she successful in picking up the whole squirrel pile, lifting it a mere inch off the ground and dragging it horizontally across the forest floor, maybe two or three yards. Tippy was able to think quickly and grab Puttermunch and tuck him snuggly under him, wrapping his tail around him to secure him, so that the baby squirrel's entire torso was bound up in tail fluff and he was kept high enough off the ground so as not to get dragged and de-furred and possibly even skinned. The owl sputtered and fluttered and nearly lost her lift. She decided to let go before crashing to the ground. It was just too much squirrel to handle. Best to go find a red-backed vole for dinner.

The squirrels unpiled themselves and went running for a hollow log lying nearby. Carrying Puttermunch on his back, Tippy went in one end and Sugarcoat went in the other, followed by Nip. Billowtail held Ivy's arm and helped her into the log, next to Tippy. Billowtail was the last to squeeze in.

"Billowtail!" Ivy gasped. "You are bleeding!"

"Oh, yes," Billowtail panted. "I got a little scratched by the talons. It's just a little abrasion."

"A little abrasion?" Tippy exclaimed. "You've got gashes all down your back."

"It's OK," Billowtail said. "It's not a cat bite. It will heal."

They all slept in the log, emerging in the dewy gray dawn, when they were certain the owl had gone to bed. Billowtail's back was still incredibly sore, but he did feel the healing process underway.

There was a painful tightness, like the skin was already growing toward itself to begin closing the gap.

"Do you think the fur will grow back?" Billowtail asked Ivy as she inspected his wounds in the light of morning.

"I'm sure it will." She gave him a reassuring smile. "You were so brave, Billowtail. You saved us all. I am sorry you have to suffer like this."

"I am happy to suffer as long as you are all safe."

"Sir Sniff would be proud," said Sugarcoat.

"Who Sir Sniff?" Puttermunch asked, running back and forth over the top of the hollow log.

"He was a—" Billowtail felt his throat start to tighten as tears threatened to choke off his answer.

"He was a great king," said Sugarcoat with characteristically perfect composure. "He gave his life for us."

Tippy, Billowtail and Nip looked at the ground, which is where squirrels look when they are suffering sadness.

"Now Puttermunch," said Sugarcoat. "Show me where you put that thread."

Puttermunch ran right to one of the ten thousand rocks near the brook, all of which looked like each other, picked it up and pulled out the thread, dangling it over his head, smiling broadly.

"Ah, to have the sharpness of youth," said Sugarcoat, "and be able to remember where you put things. You, Puttermunch, are my hero." She gave him a tight hug, took the thread and placed it around her neck. "And now, little one, it's time to go home."

CHAPTER TWENTY-FOUR

THE END OF THE WORLD

TIPPY AND NIP STAYED with Puttermunch in a tall tree while he took a nap. They vowed to stay awake, even though squirrels of all ages delight in afternoon naps. Billowtail and Ivy accompanied Sugarcoat to listen in on the Great Pinkies for clues to a route home that would by-pass the dead forest. Billowtail continually warned of getting too close so as to be noticed, so Sugarcoat decided to send him up a nearby tree to stand guard. When adequate information was obtained, Sugarcoat called Billowtail down and took his spot in the tree, saying she needed a bit of a nap.

Ivy had gathered some dandelions, and she and Billowtail took turns pulling off petals and stuffing them in their mouths.

"So much has happened," Ivy said. "So many important things. It's strange to think we won't see each other again."

"Well, we won't have to part ways for quite a while yet. We have to see you safely home, of course."

"I am not going home, Billowtail."

"You're not?" Billowtail's heart skipped at least a beat and a half at the thought of Ivy coming home with him to Bon Arbre.

"I am going on from here, Billowtail," Ivy said.

"Going on?"

"I am going to the end of the world."

"The end of the world? Why on earth would you want to go there?"

"That's where the sea is."

"At the end of the world?"

"It's not really the end of the world," Ivy explained. "Sugarcoat says that's just what the Great Pinkies call the place—Finnis Terrae. It is as far west as you can go. On land, anyway."

"And then there is the sea."

"Yes! The sea!"

"Why the sea, Ivy?"

"I cannot tell you exactly why. I just know I have to go."

"You have to go?"

"Yes, I have to. It's something I've always dreamed of. And from here, I'm already half way there."

Billowtail could not hide his sadness.

"I will miss you, Billowtail," Ivy said.

"I will miss you, Ivy."

"You can come with me, you know."

"I have been away so long." Billowtail cast his gaze on the horizon, toward the direction of home. "I have to go home now."

"Can't blame you for that, I suppose."

"Thank you, Ivy," Billowtail held out his paw and Ivy took hold of it softly. "For everything."

"Thank *you* for everything, Billowtail."

"No need to thank me. I did not do anything."

"Oh, but you did. I would have never left my tree if it wasn't for you. And I wouldn't have been part of this great adventure."

Billowtail laughed and shook his head. "I've never known a squirrel like you before. And I am quite certain that as long as I live, I shall never cross paths with another Ivy Silkpocket." That statement caused an aching in his chest, as he fully understood the truth of it.

"And you, my friend Billowtail, are an original." She took the shell from around her neck and put it around Billowtail's.

"No," he said, holding it in his hand and looking at it with wide eyes. "I can't take this."

"Sure you can," Ivy said. "I have a feeling there are an abundance of these where I am going."

"When will you leave?"

"I have to go now. Sugarcoat helped me find some Great Pinkies bound for the sea. They are leaving now. Will you say good-bye to the others for me?"

"Of course."

"Well," she bowed her head slightly, "good-bye, Billowtail."

"Ivy?" Billowtail looked down at his feet and then up into Ivy's soft eyes. "Let's not forget to remember each other."

"I will think of you whenever I look up into the night sky, at the Camino. I will be happy to ponder which specks of dust are from your feet."

Billowtail held tight to the shell as he watched Ivy Silkpocket disappear into the bushes. He saw the rustling of a leaf or two as she began her short trek back to the road where she would embark on her clandestine journey, following some unsuspecting Great Pinkies to the end of the world.

CHAPTER TWENTY-FIVE

TOWARD
THE SEA

U PON FURTHER CONSIDERATION, Sugarcoat decided it was too soon to leave Compostela. She deemed it wise to give Billowtail
some time to heal and Puttermunch time to find
his boy. He had to say good-bye. And The Alliance
had yet to see what all the pilgrims had come all
this way to see. The squirrels owed it to themselves
after all these many miles

Sugarcoat did not think it wise to bring Puttermunch inside. But Billowtail made him repeatedly
promise to be quiet and still. The Great Pinkies
might not take too kindly to having squirrels in the
Cathedral. Rodents are often scorned because they
are assumed to carry disease.

"Just stay with me, Puttermunch," Billowtail
directed. "And do what I do."

"I can do that," Puttermunch said in his de-
fault, loud tone. "But I no can do it as big as you."

"No, no, you don't have to do anything big," Billowtail said. "Actually, you need to do everything small. That's what you do in places like this. You will see. People go down on their knees when they enter. They are trying to make themselves small."

"I already small," said Puttermunch. "I be good at this."

"Yes, you are small," said Billowtail, "but your voice is very big. Make it smaller so nobody hears us. Better yet, don't talk at all. Promise?"

"I promise."

That promise lasted exactly twenty-three seconds, and then came a barrage of whispered comments and questions as the squirrels made their way along in the shadows. The shell around Billowtail's neck made it a bit difficult to maneuver nimbly, as it was quite large compared to a squirrel.

It is difficult to appreciate how odd silver and gold look to a country squirrel. There is nothing in Bon Arbre that looks remotely like it, except maybe when the sun rises or sets and floats its brilliance on the surface of a puddle or when the moon shows its entire face against the black sky. But the thing Billowtail was looking at right now at the far end of the Cathedral was not caused by the sun, nor the moon. It was standing there, sure and solid, on its own. It reminded Billowtail of the canopy of a tree, except it had no trunk to hold it up and no reason to be providing shade, since it was indoors. Under the golden canopy was a banquet table reserved for some kind of special meal. It was similar to those the squirrels had seen and Sugarcoat had learned about along the pilgrim road in all the grand buildings the Great Pinkies call churches. You could tell these places meant a great deal to the humans because they became very quiet and serious when they entered. And you could tell whoever designed them really wished people to enter because they were built with many wide doors.

Enthroned above and behind the banquet table was the likeness of St. James, in whose lap Tippy had made a full recovery. The squirrels had no way of knowing, of course, that this man would someday, for completely different reasons, be called upon as the patron saint of veterinarians.

"Look!" whispered Billowtail, pointing into the quiet crowd, gathered in the church. "Look over there!"

"The brown Great Pinky who saved me!" exclaimed Tippy in hushed excitement.

"And me," whispered Billowtail.

"And me," said Sugarcoat.

"And me!" cried Puttermunch.

The squirrels all looked at Puttermunch. "Shhh," they admonished in unison.

"When did he save you?" whispered Billowtail

"I not know when."

"Well, how then?" asked Sugarcoat.

"Outside the shop. A mean lady try to hit me with broom. He buy broom from her and smile at me."

"Ah, yes, that smile," Billowtail said.

"What's he doing?" Tippy asked. The man was down on his knees, eyes closed, facing the large gold canopy.

"He making he self very small," said Puttermunch.

He was there, motionless and quiet and small for a long, long time. The squirrels were waiting for him to leave the Cathedral, so they could follow him outside, but he just never did leave. What Billowtail would have done if he could have been in his presence once more, he was not exactly sure. He would have liked to find a way to say goodbye. And yet, good-bye didn't seem quite right. It seemed to Billowtail that their paths would cross again.

The squirrels finally left the Cathedral through one of the side doors, hoping for obscurity, since maybe it would not be as crowded outside as the main entrance had been.

"There he is!" cried Puttermunch. "There's my boy!"

Across the quiet garden, sitting on a stone bench, there indeed was the boy, his head bowed and his elbows propped on his knees. Puttermunch took off toward him, bounding in high arcs, his willowy tail drawing invisible serpentine trails on the air. The boy lowered and cupped both hands, and Puttermunch ran right into them. A smile grew wide across the boy's face. Puttermunch gave a little squeak and jumped off, scurrying back to the rosebushes where The Alliance waited. The boy noticed the four squirrels hiding there and waved.

"Looks like you're in good hands, little fellow," Sugarcoat heard him say.

"OK," Puttermunch said, looking up into Sugarcoat's eyes. "I ready now."

"Well then," Sugarcoat announced, "it seems that time has come. It's time to go home."

This news was greeted with unbridled jubilation on the part of a couple of squirrels. Nip and Tippy chased each other in celebratory circles around Billowtail, who eventually had to give up the impossible task of keeping his eye trained on the euphoric duo. It was making him dizzy. Puttermunch decided he was squirrel enough to join them and jumped headlong into the elation.

Billowtail shook his head and smiled at Sugarcoat, who watched from a short distance, propped against the trunk of a mature rose tree. "I guess they are ready," he hollered at her.

None of the three merrymakers seemed to notice when Billowtail snuck out of the circle to have a more serious conversation with Sugarcoat.

"How difficult do you think the return trip will

be?" Billowtail stood with his back propped against the adjacent side of the rose tree trunk, not looking in her direction.

"Now that we have the thread back and Puttermunch in our possession," she said with a relaxed smile, "it will be as easy as falling out of a tree."

"Do you suppose a party of three is sufficient to get Puttermunch home safely?"

"Why yes, Billowtail, but we are four. *Now* who's talking crazy?"

"Well, if three is enough, then—then—" Billowtail pretended to get distracted by the game Tippy and Nip had devised to entertain Puttermunch. The two of them were holding opposite ends of a large, fresh basswood leaf, stretched taunt between them, bouncing a perfectly-spherical rose hip on top of it.

"Then what, Billowtail?"

"Maybe it's best if I don't go home."

"Not go home?" Sugarcoat turned to look into Billowtail's face. "But there's no reason to fear going back, Billowtail. Tippy is alive, and we have rescued Puttermunch. You'll be a hero."

"I'm no hero. I'm just Billowtail. I don't even have a last name, or a family or—"

Suddenly, the frolicking stopped. Tippy and Nip froze and stared at Billowtail with wide eyes. Sometimes even squirrels forget the exceptional quality of a squirrel's sense of hearing, even when the mind is seemingly completely engaged in something else.

"No family?" Tippy looked wounded. "What about us?"

"Well, of course. You all are like family." Billowtail smiled and gave Tippy a pat on the back. "Sure. Sure you are."

"Then what is it, Billowtail?" Sugarcoat asked, fret lines on her brow.

"Don't worry, Sugarcoat. I am not running

away from anything anymore. I'm running *to* something."

"Well, then?" prompted Nip. "What is it?"

"There is something out there," Billowtail said, gazing off into the Western sky. "I have gotten a taste of it, and now I can't live without it."

"Oh," Tippy said, enlightened. "Of course. It's a vineyard, isn't it?"

"Grapes," Nip agreed. "But how will you survive the arrows?"

"No," Billowtail said softly. "It's much more than that."

"What?" Sugarcoat asked impatiently. "What is it?"

"It's soft. It's powerful. It's all-consuming like a raging fire. Yet light as a whisper on the wind."

"You poor chap, you do have it bad," said Sugarcoat. "Only a girl can turn an ordinary tree squirrel into a poet."

"No, it's not a vineyard or a girl. It's the whole reason we came after Puttermunch," Billowtail continued. "This whole journey I've been asking myself why I am here. And I finally figured it out. I came on this journey looking for something."

"Of course you did. We all came looking for something." Sugarcoat smiled as she watched Puttermunch chase his tail. "Or rather, some*one*."

"Yes, I know that's my excuse for coming. And it really is nice helping out poor Mrs. Poggins and reuniting mother and child. But there was something else to be found, besides a baby squirrel. For a long time there, I thought fate was flawed in choosing me to live instead of my brothers and sisters. Then, somewhere in this journey, I realized that maybe I had a purpose. Then, I blundered everything so badly, I was back to wondering why I had to be the one who survived. It seemed the world would be a better place without me. Then, Puttermunch was found and Tippy returned, and it became clear once more that I am here for a reason."

"Yes," agreed Sugarcoat.

"But I was wrong," Billowtail said. "Again."

"What do you mean?" said Sugarcoat. "Of course you are here for a reason. We are all here for a reason."

"What's that word the Great Pinkies have for it, Sugarcoat?" Billowtail begged. "It's just one single, simple word."

"I am sorry to say I do not know what you are talking about, Billowtail."

"It's the thing that makes the Great Pinkies do extraordinary things."

"Insanity?"

"No, no. I wish we had a word for it in Squirrelish. But, sadly, I do not think we do. But, if we did, we would use it to describe what Sir Sniff did for us."

A look of clarity came over Sugarcoat's face. "I think they call that *love*."

"Love?" Billowtail said, pensively.

"Love?" Tippy asked.

"Yes," Sugarcoat said. "I am quite certain that's the word the Great Pinkies have for such a thing."

"And, in my opinion," Billowtail said. "That's what makes them great."

"But I still don't understand why you feel you must go," Sugarcoat said. "This love the humans speak of is everywhere. Or so they say."

"Yes, but I must find my portion of it out there," he tilted his head into the setting sun. "Toward the sea."

"She left three days ago, Billowtail," Tippy said. "What are the chances of finding her now?"

"What were the chances of finding Puttermunch?" Billowtail smiled. "I will find her. I am a golden squirrel, not a green one. I have experience."

"Experience won't benefit you half as much as that soft and powerful force of which you speak, Billowtail." Sugarcoat moved close to him and placed her hand gently over his heart. "And you possess it in abundance."

Billowtail hugged Sugarcoat tight, sinking his paws into her lush white fur. Since the minute Ivy left, Billowtail could think of nothing but all the dangers that await her on the road to the sea. A squirrel should not go it alone, especially if she has never travelled before. As much as Billowtail longed for home, and would have not been at all unhappy with the hero's welcome, he could not let Ivy face all the many perils of the road by herself. But holding onto Sugarcoat now, and feeling what it might have felt like to be a mother's son, it became clear to Billowtail that love always comes at a cost.

"Do you suppose we will see you again in Bon Arbre, Billowtail?" Sugarcoat asked, loosening her embrace to look into his eyes.

"If such a thing is within my power, you will surely see me again."

Billowtail gave Nip a hug and then Tippy. Puttermunch jumped into Billowtail's arms and snuggled his face into his shoulder. Billowtail hid the twinge of pain Puttermunch's paws caused on the raw skin of his back. He set the young squirrel down gently next to Tippy and Nip. "You three boys be good now, you hear?"

Tippy hugged Billowtail around the midsection again and sniffled. "If I knew his name, I would call for my eagle friend right now, to snatch you and carry you home."

Billowtail chuckled. "I may need that someday." He picked up the shell around his neck and ran his forefinger along one of its grooves. Sugarcoat had told him of the things she had learned about the shell by listening to pilgrims at the Cathedral. The shell is many things to a pilgrim. It is a scoop for drinking water. It is a bowl for holding food. It is a signal to other pilgrims that they are not alone on the road. It is a symbol of St. James, born of a legend, which you shall perhaps hear one day. With grooves wrought by the ocean, the shell is a map, marked with all the routes from far-off places, converging at a single point. It contains, carved within it, both the journey and the destination.

And these things all made sense to Billowtail when he heard them. He was not even a little tempted to think Sugarcoat was losing her mind.

"Yes, someday, my dear friend Tippy Whimtucket, I may wish for a ride home." Billowtail pressed the shell's ridges into the palm of his hand. "But at the moment, I've got everything I need."

About the Author

Sherry Boas is author of the highly-acclaimed Lily Series, which began with *Until Lily* and has grown into an expanding collection of novels whose characters' lives are unpredictably transformed by a woman with Down syndrome. The latest in the series is the fourth book, *The Things Lily Knew*.

Boas is also author of *A Mother's Bouquet: Rosary Meditations for Moms* and the novel, *Wing Tip*, a story about a Catholic priest whose mother's death-bed confession reveals a startling family secret.

Little Maximus Myers is Boas' first children's book. It tells the story of an unusually small altar boy who has a profound revelation about the beauty of his smallness while struggling to carry the cross in the procession at Mass.

Boas is owner of Caritas Press, publisher of a series of rosary meditations for moms, dads, children, teens, grandparents and altar servers.

Although she won numerous awards in her ten-year career as a journalist for a daily newspaper before her children were born, it was her vocation as a mother that would best prepare her for an author's career. For her, truth resounds and inspiration abounds in the struggles and triumphs of everyday family life. She and her husband, Phil, are the joyful, special needs, adoptive parents of four warm-hearted and highly-adrenalized human beings, who make life rich beyond belief. They live in Arizona.

You can find Boas' work at **LilyTrilogy.com, CaritasPress.org, CatholicWord.com** and in Catholic book stores nationwide. Also on Facebook: Sherry Boas Fan Page.

FOR UPDATES FROM SHERRY BOAS
and THE ALLIANCE
VISIT BILLOWTAIL.COM